SMALL ETERNITIES

ACKNOWLEDGEMENTS
I would like to thank my old friend Maggie B, currently of Ontario and
Florida, for allowing Larissa Underwood to appropriate her squirrel story.
The extract in French from Marie Underwood's diary is a quote from
Arthur Rimbaud's prose poem *Les Ponts*, c.1875.

ORCHARD BOOKS
96 Leonard Street, London EC2A 4XD
Orchard Books Australia
32/45-51 Huntley Street, Alexandria, NSW 2015
ISBN 1 84121 168 0
First published in Great Britain in 2004
Text © Michael Lawrence 2004
The right of Michael Lawrence to be identified as the author
of this work has been asserted by him in accordance with the
Copyright, Designs and Patents Act, 1988.
A CIP catalogue record for this book is available from the British Library.
1 3 5 7 9 10 8 6 4 2
Printed in Great Britain

MICHAEL LAWRENCE

SMALL ETERNITIES

[handwritten signature]

[handwritten] Sept. 16, 2004

PART TWO OF
THE ALDOUS LEXICON

ORCHARD BOOKS

DEDICATION

*My grandfather was a thin, serious man whose hand,
as a very young child, I was proud to hold.
My grandmother, plump and jolly, supremely competent,
was the heart and soul of everything, loved by everyone
who knew her. These two were the foundation of my
early life, just as their ivy-covered riverside house provided
the landing stage for all that followed.*
Small Eternities *is dedicated to the memory of Selina and
Charles Lawrence, who started the whole damn business.*

AUTHOR'S NOTE

The Aldous Lexicon *is a continuous narrative in three volumes.
Confusion might arise if these three are read in anything other
than chronological order, which is: A CRACK IN THE LINE;
SMALL ETERNITIES; THE UNDERWOOD SEE.*

You, if you were sensible,
When I tell you the stars flash signals, each one dreadful,
You would not turn and answer me
'The night is wonderful.'

What thing better are you, what worse?
What have you to do with the mysteries
Of this ancient place, of my ancient curse?
What place have you in my histories?

D.H. Lawrence: Under the Oak, 1916

One October afternoon, when I was twenty-four and 3000 miles from home, a new friend of mine, a psychiatrist's son from Palo Alto, California, stood up suddenly and read out this poem, in full. Although there were others in the room he addressed the lines to me, for his own unexpressed reasons. The poem, cavalierly truncated here, did not find its way back to me until I'd finished work on this book. In its entirety it seems to me startlingly prescient.

Michael Lawrence

Part Three
LEGACY OF A POET

THE YEARS BETWEEN

PRELUDE

Aldous was just six years old when he first began to wonder where they would bury him, and when. Every bedtime for as long as he could remember, his mother had made him kneel with folded hands and closed eyes and pray for the continued well-being of every relative he could think of. And when he'd dealt with the entire company he was always to finish with: 'And please, Lord, see me safely through the night and let me live to see another day.' Every morning he woke nervously, wondering if he was still alive. He always was, of course, but as the years wore on it never ceased to seem unlikely that God would always be so generous.

Worries about his own mortality were far from his mind the day he saw the boat, however. It was June. He was eleven. Because of the flooding the family had been forced upstairs, which meant that he spent more time in his room than usual. This was fine with him. The situation, like the view, was a singular novelty. And this time there was something extra. On going to his window for the umpteenth time that day, he saw an empty rowing boat bobbing gently, just beyond the landing stage. He leant out to peer as far to right and left as the willows would allow. There was no one in the water. No one he could see. Curious!

He ran in search of his mother; found her in the spare bedroom, rearranging it as a temporary sitting room. She wasn't in the best of humours (all the bother, the devastation downstairs) but he told her what he'd seen, drew her by the hand to his room, his window. They looked out, side-by-side. There was no sign of the boat.

'But it *was* there,' he insisted, as though accused of lying.

His mother smiled. 'I'm sure it was, cherie. But it's gone now.'

And as far as Marie Underwood was concerned that was the end of it. But not for Aldous. His imagination took flight. Had someone fallen out of the boat and drowned? Was there a body caught in the lilies or the reeds? Had it floated away? Would it end up in someone's garden, under a bridge, in the flooded market square at Stone?

The mystery of the empty boat was such that it might

have bothered him intermittently for week afterwards –
months – if events had not driven it and other matters
from his mind.

Events. Visitors. That death of his.

Part One
VOICES, SOMETIMES

SUNDAY

Sunday: 1

The rains had been heavier than predicted by the ash-blonde pundits, and lasted longer than expected, causing the river to swell and burst its banks, the consequence being the worst flooding in half a century or more. Entrepreneurs had immediately started going round with sandbags which, pressed against doors, kept all but the merest dribble out. There were two main doors at Withern Rise, and three sets of French windows. All were sealed, but the garage doors were forgotten until it was too late. By the time Ivan remembered, the floor of the car was under water and he was convinced that it would never work again. According to the local TV news, insurance companies were bracing themselves for the claims that were going to 'flood in'. The pun amused the presenters smirking in tandem behind their shared desk.

'Smug bastards,' Ivan muttered.

But the rain had stopped at last, sometime in the night, and Naia, gleefully out of doors for the first time in days, took photos of the submerged garden before setting off in Grandpa Rayner's old green waders. Rayner hadn't been a tall man, and he'd had small feet, so she could only just get into them, and they pinched her toes, but at least they kept her dry as the water sloshed around her legs. She wanted to see this new 'landscape' from the pedestrian bridge that rose like a long, low rainbow drained of colour to link the drowned Coneygeare with the drowned Meadows. It was quite a slog up the slope in those boots, but the view from the top was worth it: a wide world of water punctuated by tiled and chimneyed arks, the floating spires of churches, sunken trees in clusters. Withern could not be seen from the bridge, largely thanks to the enormous willow, in full bright leaf, at the southern end of the landing stage. But she was delighted to see a pair of swans cruising serenely by.

There was no empty rowing boat on Naia's river. Not then.

•

Sunday: 2

Alaric had never known such contentment. For four months he had complained about nothing, longed for nothing, not once wished for more than he had. He no longer slouched around, scowling and snapping at the world. Why should he? His life was complete. Best of all, the real prize, he had his mother back. Well, as good as. He was able, for long stretches, to forget that she had given birth to Naia, not him. Naia's former occupation of this life presented him with a few problems, however. Her brain held the memories that were expected to be in his: conversations, incidents, jokes, shared sights and sounds. There'd been a lot of odd looks and raised eyebrows, from his teachers, from Alex and Ivan, his friends, but these were generally overcome without too much hassle.

His relationship with his friends was curious, even to him. *Especially* to him. As he hadn't set foot in this reality before February, let alone been absorbed into it so that it seemed to everyone that he'd always been here, the boys who thought of him as their mate had no idea that they hadn't previously known anyone called Alaric. They wouldn't have been pally with Naia, or any girl, except under sufferance, or unless she was a 'goer' like Bonnie the Bike. One or two of them might have fancied her – Davy Raine, for one – but most were more likely to catcall as she walked by, or raise a fist while thumping the crook of an arm, leering for one another's benefit.

Naia. She was never far from his mind. She was the twin he would have liked. If they had in fact been twins they would have argued a lot, but they would always have made up before long because, deep down, they were so much in tune. She was livelier than him, with a quicker smile, a lighter, brighter character, yet they were the same in most ways that mattered. But they were not twins. In a way, because of their exchanged circumstances, they were enemies now. It had not been his intention, but he had seized her world, literally, and occupied it today as if born into it. She no longer had a place here. But Alaric harboured a secret dread, which sometimes woke him in the night in a cold sweat, that Naia might find a way to return here and repossess her life: a recurrent fear which he suppressed for large tracts of time, but which never quite went away.

Now that the rain had stopped, he wanted to go out and experience the new conditions. Question was, how was he supposed to walk across a flooded garden, and beyond? The only boots long enough were Grandpa Rayner's old waders, but they were too small in the foot. Which left…shorts and sandals. Sandals! What the hell was he doing with sandals in this reality? Still, they'd serve a purpose. The water would be cold on his legs, but he could put up with that for a while.

He told Alex of his intention. To her face he called her 'Mum', as she would expect, but in his mind he used her name. He'd never done this with his real mother. Ivan, too, was 'Dad' only when addressed. Alaric had tried to overcome this last small hurdle of acceptance, but so far he hadn't been able to manage it. In time, perhaps.

'Well mind how you go,' Alex had said when he told her of his intention. 'A person can drown in two inches of water, you know.'

'Leave off, Mum, I'm nearly seventeen.'

'It doesn't matter how old you are, it could still happen.'

'I promise not to drown, all right?'

'You're not going to the village, are you?'

'I was going to the long bridge, to see what it all looks like.'

'If you were, I could do with some things from Mr and Mrs Paine's.'

'It's the wrong way from the bridge.'

'All right. I'll go out myself later.'

He hesitated. She wanted him to go to the village shop. How could he refuse? Once upon a time, yes, before the accident that had taken her from him, but not now she was back. He could refuse her nothing now.

'What do you want?'

She brightened. 'I have a list.'

He followed her to the kitchen, where she handed him a list of items, four of which were either heavy (washing powder and rinse) or bulky (toilet rolls and kitchen towels).

'I can't carry all these!'

'Well get what you can. I'd be glad of the washing powder. If I don't do a decent wash soon we'll have nothing to wear.'

'What does it matter?' he said. 'We're not going anywhere while it's like this.'

'That's not the point.'

'Seems a fair point to me.'

It was true about them not going far while the flood conditions lasted. They had no transport, Ivan couldn't open the shop because Stone High Street was full of water, the classes Alex ran at the College had been cancelled, and Alaric's school was closed for the duration. He wasn't too dismayed by the last of these, because it meant a break from the dreaded GCSEs. He thought he was doing quite well in the exams – a hell of a lot better than he would have done in his old reality, where his life had been conducted from within a fog of self-pity and resentment – but that didn't mean he was enjoying them.

With the external doors barricaded against the flood, he had no choice but to climb out of a ground-floor window. About to do so, he heard Alex say, behind him: 'I'm going to go through everything again. I'm *determined* to find that photo album. Such a mystery where it's got to.'

'Good luck,' he said, hoisting a leg over the ledge and lowering himself into the water.

Sunday: 3

Aldous remembered strolling about the garden and the village with Grandpa Eldon, arm raised to hold his hand. Grandpa's palm had felt like stretched velvet. They'd had a goat then: a handsome white nanny called Flo. Allowed to wander freely round the grounds, Flo did an excellent job of keeping the grass down, but because she would eat virtually anything, the vegetable and flower gardens had had to be fenced off. Flo, too, was attached to Eldon Underwood, and trotted to him whenever she saw him. When he and his little grandson walked round the garden, Flo kept her jealous distance. Then came a day when she could restrain herself no longer. She charged at Aldous from behind, lifted him on her horns, sent him flying onto the gravel path. Eldon, in a fury, locked the goat in the shed. Next day, men came and took her away. Even all these years after the event, Aldous was sorry about that. He'd never dared go too near the beautiful animal, but he'd loved to see her tripping around the garden, nibbling whatever was within reach, standing on her hind hooves to reach a batch of leaves or thorns or berries. But that was a long time ago. Grandpa Eldon had died when Aldous was five years old.

If Eldon Underwood had still been about he would almost certainly have accompanied his son and eldest grandson to the village for provisions, delighting in the adventure of rowing there. His son's name was Alaric Eldon, known to all but his wife and children, a few of his employees and most tradesmen, as A.E. Born at Withern Rise, growing up beside the river, it had seemed to A.E. Underwood the most natural thing in the world for him to become a boat-builder. He had started out as apprentice to J. Rickles and Sons of Eaton Fane, but for the past fourteen years had had his own yard just along the river from Withern Rise.

The boat they were taking to the village was not one of A.E.'s finest, but it was a serviceable enough craft. It was, however, too broad to pass through the side gate, so they rowed along the drive to the main entrance. Rowing where they usually walked amused them. Aldous's mother would not have been amused. They'd been living upstairs since the water burst into the house, and Marie Underwood, gazing despairingly down from the landing, had never ceased to fret about the damage. Every downstairs room was flooded; the carpets, furnishings and wallpaper would be ruined. A.E. was as aware of this as anyone, but he was a light-hearted man who took most domestic tribulations in his stride. Some might have said that he could afford to. His yard had never been busier than in the last five years, thanks to fat government contracts for small boats.

Today, the view from the gate, which should have been of the broad portion of common land known as the Coneygeare, was not of land at all, but of water specked with craft similar to theirs. The chance to go boating on the Coneygeare was not to be passed up.

'Mr Knight!' A.E. shouted to the occupant of one boat. 'Isn't it about time you attended to my lawns?'

The other man laughed. 'I'll need diving gear, Mister.'

His employer made a scowl. 'You'll not be mollycoddled by me, sir!'

And the two boats passed with much good humour.

Sunday: 4

From the crest of the bridge, Naia contemplated the great lake that covered Withy Meadows to her left, swallowed the river before her, and reached all across the Coneygeare to her right. There was no question of attempting a foray into the Meadows, where the water was so high in parts that the benches were reduced to strips of floating wood, while shorter and younger trees lacked trunks. She was tempted to wade across the Coneygeare, however. She started down the slope of the bridge, the way she'd just come, but paused half way, projecting ahead to a possibility that seemed to her little short of certainty. When she stood still, or strolled on open ground, Naia looked rather elegant, with her broad shoulders, her impressive height, long auburn hair. Boys admired her – until they saw her in a hurry, especially running, when her arms refused to stay anywhere near her sides and her legs became poorly jointed stilts. Wading across such a great expanse of water suddenly seemed too much of a risk. Even at a measured pace, she would surely miss her footing at some stage, plunge face down, or backwards with flailing arms, to splutter to her feet, hair in eyes, clothes clinging, dignity blown. She continued her descent of the bridge and, instead, turned homeward, but reaching Withern's gate she found herself reluctant to go indoors so soon, and went on, turning left after a few paces, towards the old cemetery that paralleled the house.

The cemetery, being slightly raised, was less affected by the flooding than many other parcels of land thereabouts. All graves that were not further elevated were under water, but every stone and monument and marker stood clear save for a few centimetres at the base. Naia took some pictures, but when her lens turned to the wall that described the eastern boundary of Withern Rise, she put her camera away. Here, under this weathered old wall, was the grave she spent a lot of time trying not to think about. Much of the headstone was concealed by ivy, and tall weeds had grown around it since her last visit a couple of months ago. Ashamed of herself for neglecting it, she went over and pulled the ivy away; tore the weeds from the water, cast them aside in anger. *How dare they grow here?* But as she worked to clear the area, anger was displaced by a very different emotion, and when she straightened up her eyes, like the grave, were flooded. Then the tears were spurting, shoulders shaking, as she gave in, as she did all too rarely outside of her room, to the misery of her situation, the horrible injustice of it all.

For four interminable months she had struggled daily through the creaking aftermath of the fatal quirk that had dumped her in this false reality. False to her anyway. It was as real to everyone else here – the few she knew, the billions she did not – as her original reality had been to her. There, beyond reach or contact, her mother still lived. Here, she lay beneath this stone, this water, amid these eager weeds. The cut-off had been as swift, and as total, as it had been unexpected, and there was no way to reverse things, no way back. The sheer awfulness of that was bad enough, but she was stung by guilt too. Guilt that she hadn't told her mother that she loved her in the final days, or shown her the kind of affection that might (in normal family circumstances) cause a fond smile in quiet moments. At times, the guilt hurt almost as much as the loss itself.

For Naia, these past months, there'd been much private weeping and a deal of public acting in the cause of thwarting suspicions that she might not be who people took her for. The greatest pity of her life here, bereavement aside, was that there was no one to talk to about the things that really mattered. There were several ready-made friends, some of whom she'd not been friendly with in the old reality, or even known. One or two considered themselves 'close', as their counterparts had actually been close. She went through the motions with these few, but always with a measure of reserve (occasionally remarked upon) because she knew, as they did not, that until February they hadn't even heard of her.

It took a supreme effort to regain control of herself, but as she blinked the last of the tears away Naia sensed that she was no longer quite alone. Glancing around, she saw a figure in black, an old man, turn in the water-filled lane below the steps. She knew him. She'd spoken to him once, in this very place, her first full day in this reality, when she had again been in tears. He'd given his name, a name that had made no sense until, some time afterwards, she had come to terms with the fact that her life had altered beyond recognition, and that anything was possible, anything at all, even the unimaginable.

Sunday: 5

The shopping done and delivered, Alaric went for a wade with some of the lads. He and Mick Chilton were the only ones in shorts. The others made no concessions to the flooding, preferring to put up with wet clothes than to seem bothered by discomfort. One of his friends here was Gus O'Brien, who believed he'd known him since they were six. If there'd been a Gus O'Brien in Alaric's previous reality they'd never met. Even the friends who were essentially the same here were slightly changed, not in looks but in some of their mannerisms, attitudes, habits. He'd known a Davy Raine and a Paul Kearley in the old reality, but the present Davy swore a lot more, and this Paul had a sort of nervous tick in his left eye which the other Paul (whose step-dad didn't get plastered and knock him about) had not. The new Mick Chilton wasn't much different from the old, but Mick's memories of the things they'd got up to together were fictions to Alaric. In his former reality, Chilton had been a fairly peripheral figure, with different pals. There, Leonard Paine had been Alaric's closest friend, but here there was no Leonard Paine. No Len Paine! No Lenny! In the old reality Mr and Mrs Paine, who ran the corner shop in both Eynesfords, had three sons, with Len the eldest. Here, they had two sons and a daughter named Shallan. Like Len previously, Shallan was in his class. Len and Shallan Paine: counterparts of him and Naia. He imagined they were as unaware of one another as he and Naia had been before their paths first crossed on the second anniversary of his mother's death.

Distracted by thoughts such as these, Alaric hadn't been paying attention to the row that had flared up between Paul and Mick. But he noticed when they threw themselves bodily at one another, hit the water together, went under, came up wrestling and punching. Then Mick got Paul's neck in an armlock and shoved his face under. He would have held it there if the others hadn't hauled him off. After that they simmered down, looked for other diversions.

They were too old to use the play area, but there were no kids about, and no adults to give them grief. Besides, as they saw it the flood had washed many of the old rules away, for the time being at least. So they spun the roundabout and flung themselves upon it, splashed up and down on the seesaws, and swept down the slide into the water, to rise effing and blinding and spluttering.

'Look at him!' Gus said suddenly.

They all turned. It was the old man Alaric had first seen across the river from his bedroom in his former reality, and a couple of times since, here. Two variations of the same man, obviously. The reason Gus pointed him out wasn't merely that he was of a much older generation (and thus ripe for derision) but that, wading across the Coneygeare in their general direction, his overcoat floated about him like a great black cloak.

'Old loon,' said Mick.

'Nutter,' said Davy.

'Who is he?' Alaric asked, displaying less interest than he felt.

Nobody knew. Nobody gave a monkey's. A couple of them had seen him about, but that was it.

Because an adult was approaching, even a fruitcake like this one, Davy, Paul, Mick and Gus returned to their play with a touch less verve and clamour. Alaric took to one of the swings and pushed himself back and forth, heels skimming the water, keeping a sly eye on the man as he drew near. Where could he be going? Surely not over the bridge, into the Meadows which were completely under water. But soon it was obvious that he was indeed approaching the bridge. Passing within twenty metres of the boys, he glanced their way.

'What you lookin' at?' Paul shouted.

'Piss off!' bawled Mick.

'Tosser,' said Gus, more quietly.

If offended, he didn't show it. He raised a hand as if to mates of his own, and started up the slope. He'd only gone a short distance, however, when he paused, half turned, looked at Alaric. Just him, not the others. Mick noticed.

'He fancies you, Al. Old perve.'

The man continued up the bridge, and it came to them, each in turn, privately, that they were no longer enjoying the larking about, the water, the company. Time to split. Paul, Mick and Davy climbed over the play area's low barrier fence, from water into water.

'Coming?' Gus said to Alaric.

'Yeah.'

As they waded after the others, Alaric glanced back. The bridge was empty. The man had disappeared. He stopped as though slapped.

'Whassup?' Gus asked.

'That man...'

Gus looked. Was also stunned. 'Uh?'

They could see the whole bridge from there, and a great deal of the Meadows on the opposite bank. Twenty seconds earlier, the man hadn't even reached the half-way point, yet there was no sign of him now. There was nowhere, absolutely nowhere, he could have gone.

Alaric stooped to see below the bridge. 'Might have fallen over.'

'No chance,' Gus said. 'The sides are too high for us. Bloke his age wouldn't get half a leg up.'

With that he shrugged it off – who cared? – and went after the others. Alaric followed too, but slowly. He couldn't dismiss the vanishing act so easily. It was several minutes before his mind let it go. Until much later, in bed, when it returned to haunt him.

Sunday: 6

The water that had washed through the house and reached into every nook and cranny of the ground floor gave off an odour that might have been sweeter, but Marie's were the only nostrils that were offended by it. The children barely noticed, and Father had nothing to say about it. A.E. had brought a small coracle indoors, which he paddled along the hall and into the lower rooms, collecting the various bits and pieces and edibles demanded by his wife. There was only room in the little craft for him and a few things at a time, delivered to the reaching hands on the stairs. The children would have loved to join him, but it amused them to see him spinning into this room or that. Marie fretted that she was denying her children nourishing food, but for them, sandwiches made with stale bread and beef dripping added to the thrill of it all. Nor did they mind being restricted to the top of the house. Ursula and Mimi got the most out of the experience. They were great jokers, these two; incorrigible gigglers. Ray, a fragile seven-year-old, joined in their games with some enthusiasm, but Aldous, as the eldest, felt that he should be above hiding in box rooms and under beds and pretending the bath was a boat lost at sea. Besides, he preferred to fiddle with his stamp album, particularly since the arrival of a new set from Cousin Edwin in Weymouth. Exciting depictions of war planes and aircraft carriers.

Aldous had the corner bedroom, which overlooked the river from one window, the south garden from the other. It wasn't a large room, but he would have no other. He loved the way the light spilled in from two directions, tangling shadows. Not much sun at the moment, but the rain clouds had gone and the sky was brightening little by little, illuminating the fascinating new world around the house. He longed to be out there, on the wide water, exploring. The trip to the village with Father had been very enjoyable, but he wanted to go out alone at least once before the land returned, row and row and row through this strange new waterscape, returning only for tea. His father might not mind him going alone, but Maman would be far less keen. Marie Underwood worried about her children, to excess. Aldous waited until she and his father were together before broaching the subject. As expected, his mother was horrified.

'Go out *alone*? In the boat? In *this*?'

'I'll be very careful,' he said.

'There is no possibility of it,' she replied. 'None whatsoever.'

'I wonder where he was thinking of going,' his father said mildly.

'It doesn't matter where. He's not going, and there's an end to it.'

'Oh, come on, Marie. He's a good boatman. He'll come to no harm.'

Marie became imperious. 'No means no, Alaric. Is my English not *clear* enough for you?'

A.E. was not intimidated. He winked at his son. 'Leave her to me,' the wink said. 'Leave her to me.'

Sunday: 7

Apart from the willow tree and the steep grey slope of the garage roof, which between them framed the view, all that could be seen of the north garden was water. The window seat in the master bedroom had been one of her mother's favourite places. Had been, still was, she knew. In Naia's old reality Mum could often be found here, reading, drawing, dreaming. Might be sitting here this very minute, she thought, and sighed, almost content for once. The contentment wasn't entirely due to the idea that she might be sharing the view with her lost mother. A purring cat, which she stroked absently, sprawled drowsily in her lap.

It was barely more than a kitten really, this small beast. A present from Mr Knight, the gardener. He'd only been helping out for a couple of weeks when he approached her with it under his jacket. 'One of Schrödinger's offspring,' he said, revealing the perky white face.

'Schrödinger?'

'My cat. Curious beast who gets into the most unlikely scrapes, often seems to be in two places at once, or none at all. I suspect this one will be a chip off the furry old block. He's yours if you want him. If you're allowed.'

She'd been startled when Mr Knight turned up here. She'd known a version of him back home (as she often referred to the reality she'd been born into). He'd been helping in the garden there since January. But not here. It was mid-April before this reality's Mr Knight knocked on the door to offer his services, part-time. Kate wouldn't have been looking forward to tackling the enormous garden on her own even if it had been cared for. As it hadn't been touched for over two years, she almost fell into Mr Knight's arms with relief.

The cat stirred in her lap. Her stroking hand had paused and admonishing green eyes were glaring up at her: *Did I tell you to stop?* She resumed her stroking. The eyes closed. Naia returned her gaze to the view, but in those few seconds her contentment had given way to extreme regret. She would never look into her mother's eyes again. She could look a cat in the eye, but not her own mother. Worse, her mother would never give her a passing thought. The daughter she'd given birth to had been erased from her memory. Naia wondered if she existed in her mother's subconscious, an ephemeral, drifting figure; or, for that matter, if she was ever dreamt about. But even if the living Alex Underwood dreamt of her, when she woke, went to the bathroom, down for breakfast, into another day of her life, any lingering image conjured by the night would soon dissolve.

From there, Naia's thoughts turned to the one who'd taken her place in her mother's affections. Alaric. For a moment she hated him. But it passed. It wasn't his fault. He too would have had to make huge adjustments, act as if he'd always been there, pretend that the people who claimed to know him were equally familiar to him. She knew what that was like. It was because she refused to blame Alaric, and because she never expected to see him again, that she'd had his name engraved on the young cat's name-tag. It had felt odd at first, saying that name out loud when referring to a cat, but like most things she was getting used to it. In a way it was a kind of slow exorcism. Another six months, a year, and she might have virtually forgotten where the name came from.

Another year! Her stomach knotted. How could she live another year without her mother? A whole year, and the first of many. It was more than she could bear. And she didn't. Tears came for the second time in hours. Four months of holding them in, and suddenly –

'You like that seat, don't you?'

She dashed a hand across her cheeks, half turned.

'Best in the house. You don't mind...?'

Kate Faraday was a cheerful thirty-eight-year-old of medium height, with fairish brown hair which she disparagingly referred to as 'mousy'. She didn't look at all like Naia, but when they were out together they were often taken for mother and daughter, simply because they were together and a generation apart. Such mistakes pleased Kate, but while Naia was very fond of her, Kate was not her mother and she didn't want people assuming that she was.

'How can I mind? I'm the cuckoo in the nest.' Pause. 'What are you looking at?'

Leaning down to peer over Naia's shoulder, Kate noticed the shine on her cheek. Sat down beside her.

'You all right?'

'Yeah. Just having a moment. You know.'

'If there's anything...'

Naia touched the back of her hand: a simple gesture appreciated by Kate, who had her own insecurities. The cat rang his bell. *Stroke!*

'Oh, leave off, Alaric,' Naia said. 'You get quite enough attention.'

And for once it was the cat's name, the cat's alone; nothing to do with the boy who'd usurped her life.

•

Sunday: 8

'My name is Aldous Underwood and I'm seventy-one years old.' It had become his personal mantra, chanted quietly on waking each morning, and spontaneously when out and about during the day. Seventy-one. At least, that's what his birth certificate told him, measured against dates on present-day newspapers. He carried his birth certificate at all times. If he'd had more possessions this would have been his most valued. It proved he existed. The proof was for himself. He needed such evidence because his mind and his body told him different stories. Because of the way he looked he was expected to behave in an 'elderly' fashion, but this he found difficult. He practised talking seriously, walking ponderously, being long-faced when he saw the kind of everyday things – a flock of geese in the sky, a squirrel in a tree, sunshine on water – that most mature adults did not respond to. But it wasn't easy.

He had little money, the dregs of a trust fund set up by his mother a lifetime ago, but his wants were few. It was by choice that he lived out of doors, in the thicket on the opposite bank from Withern Rise. It wasn't a comfortable existence, especially now, with the flooding, but he had no complaints. He was alive again, that was what mattered. When he first came back it was winter and he'd slept on an old mattress from a nearby ditch. He'd waited till dark before dragging the mattress into the thicket, knowing that such an activity might be frowned upon by people who preferred roofs over their heads. The ground was hard back then. Ice-hard. Snow had begun to fall. Soon it had covered everything. If not for his thick overcoat and some large sheets of cardboard, also from the ditch, he would have frozen to death. His roof then, as now, was an old tent, opened out and stretched between branches. In the early weeks the nights, infinitely cold, had seemed endless, but he hadn't minded. He was glad to shiver and feel, be kept awake by discomfort. Staying awake while others slept was a rare luxury.

He'd found the hammock about two months ago, on the council tip. It was slightly stained, and it ponged a bit, but it was made of strong canvas, there were no holes in it, and the metal rings along the reinforced ends were intact. Also, importantly, it was dry. The hammock had turned out to be quite a memory-jogger. Surprised to find that he knew how to hang a hammock at all, he was fixing it in place when he recalled one they'd had when he was young in body as well as mind. It wasn't heavy canvas like this one, but of thick rope, with brass hooks. They always took it in during the winter months, but it hung in the south garden, between the apple tree and the pear, all spring and summer long, and much of the autumn. He remembered reaching up as a small boy, gripping the sides of the hammock, trying to haul himself into it, succeeding only in swinging beneath it, to the family's amusement. He managed not to swing beneath the canvas hammock, but getting into it was often a problem. Still, he managed, and there, some way above the ground, sheltered by the stretched tent, he felt safe, and a little excited. It was an adventure, like sleeping in the garden at Withern Rise, in the other hammock, on warm summer nights. Warm summer nights were yet to occur this year. The floods, dampening everything, kept temperatures in check.

Until recently Aldous had spent a good part of every day walking round the village and the town, and further afield, clutching at bits of memory triggered by some sight or sound or smell, trying to put them in context and sequence. Then the rains came, great grey walls of water, falling relentless day after day after day. He'd stayed in his shelter for longer than he liked, venturing forth only to buy bread, cheese, the odd piece of fruit that hadn't been available, even heard of, when he lived at Withern Rise. There had also been the necessary trips to the public toilets in the car-park across the area they called Withy Meadows these days: osier beds in his time. When the river spilled over the banks and continued to rise, he was glad that he'd hitched the hammock so high. Even with his weight, it remained some inches above the surface of the water. Getting out was the least pleasant aspect of using it in time of flood, but he managed, often laughing at himself, his efforts. He was alive and awake, and here. He felt privileged.

Sunday: 9

That evening, Naia's former parents got into a scrap. It wasn't a row as such; more a few rounds of tetchy backbiting. It all started with Ivan grumbling yet again about the three-and-a-half-year-old Saab in the garage. Ivan was fond of that car. It was the first he'd ever owned, apart from the forty-year-old Daimler inherited from his father.

'Yes, we know it's waterlogged,' Alex said through her teeth. 'We know it will take an eternity to dry out. We know that even *after* an eternity it may never work properly again. We know, we know, we know. You don't have to keep *saying* it.'

'It's all right for you,' Ivan said. 'It's not your car.'

'Oh? I thought it was the family car.'

'It is, but I drive it most of the time. *Used* to drive it, that is, before—'

'Ivan, will you shut up about the sodding car?' Alex said.

'You don't understand,' he wailed plaintively.

'Don't understand? How could I fail to understand when I keep hearing the same thing, hour after hour? We all have problems. We didn't ask to be flooded out. I can't get to the village without dressing like a deep-sea diver, I can't work because the College is closed, it's a constant battle to keep the water from dribbling under the doors. But you don't hear me droning on and on about it all the time.'

'What are you doing now then?' Ivan said.

'Responding,' she snapped.

This would have been an ideal time for Ivan to shut up before tempers got really frayed, but the truth was he was bored without the shop to go to, customers to chat to, stock to seek out and haggle over. Bored and therefore restless. Restless, therefore short-tempered. Short-tempered, therefore combative. So they went on, the pair of them, sniping and snarling, criticising one another with some justification and with none, spinning the whole thing out far beyond its natural span as a mere spat, until Ivan noticed that Alaric had turned the television down and was observing all this with a grin on his face.

'What's so funny?'

'You two.'

'We're not funny.'

'Are from where I'm sitting.'

'It's your mother,' Ivan said.

'What's his mother?' demanded Alex.

'You started it.'

'No I didn't. You were going on and on about your perishing car. I told you to give it a rest, that's all.'

'How can I give it a rest? It was a nice car. Now it's junk.'

'There you go again.'

'I'm just stating a fact.'

'Consider it stated and change the subject. Better still say nothing. I'm sick of the sound of your voice.'

'Oh, charming.'

'Well.'

'I mean what a thing to say.'

'You can't stop, can you?'

'I will if you will.'

'I have stopped. Just don't mention the rotten car again.'

'Rotten's the word for it now.'

'There you go again.'

'There *you* go again.'

And on they went, and on and on and on, neither of them quite able to put an end to it, concede defeat. Alaric shook his head with pleasure, as if watching two children squabbling. It was so normal. Normal and everyday. Perfect.

Later, he stood at his bedroom window overlooking

the south garden. It was growing dark, but he'd not turned the light on and could make out the Family Tree without straining. Once, long before his time, the grand old oak had been just one tree among several. Now it rose solitarily from the water, imposing in its breadth and fullness, its nearest neighbour a bank of rhododendrons and camellias. He hadn't thought about the tree much lately. His attention had been drawn by so many other things. But there was something about it that compelled him to look at it now. Almost at once a reason appeared in the figure that dropped down from it. A small silent splash and the visitor was standing in the water. Alaric leant closer to the glass. A stranger climbing out of a tree in your garden would have been startling enough, worrying enough, but...

His mouth dried. The visitor wading towards the house was close enough to recognise now. As if there could have been any doubt, even at a distance! It was him. Himself. Alaric.

The Alaric in the garden glanced up. He stopped, leant forward, trying to make out the face of the watcher at the window. Then, seeing who it was, he jumped as though struck, stumbled in the water, cast about him with something like alarm, and vanished.

MONDAY

Monday: 1

Withern Rise had become a great tri-roofed ark adrift in a tideless ocean dotted with islands composed of bushes and trees and hints of distant buildings. In his eleven years Aldous had seen his world transformed by snow, rimmed with frost, haunted by a high moon; but never had he seen it like this. He was particularly taken with the view from his room of the forest of floating willows, the osier beds.

Once, when he was little, Grandpa Eldon had persuaded the osier cutters to take him out with them. It had amused them that such a young child wanted to see them at work. Four boats had started out, with Aldous in the third, divining smooth courses through the multitude of narrow channels. Unlike him, the men did not sit. Nor did they often duck. Propelling their boats with endless poles, they bent and swayed and wove to avoid the flailing willow strings. The water had a slightly stagnant smell, but to Aldous it was part of the adventure. And what an adventure! He'd admired the osier cutters from the first time he saw them in the distance: lean standing heroes propelling their boats through waterways that few others could have navigated with ease. That day he had watched in awe as Mr Welborne, in whose boat he travelled, caught bundle after bundle of withies in a hooked pole and deftly trimmed them with knife or shears before casting them to the shallow floor of the boat.

Since that day, Aldous had never ceased to believe that if he was allowed to grow to manhood he too would become an osier cutter. He imagined himself, standing tall in a boat of his own, sleeves rolled up past the elbow, red scratches and weals on his forearms, as certain of his routes, assured in his skill, as the men he'd gone out with that day when he was small. If Maman could be persuaded to let him take the boat out he might row across the river into the forest and pretend as he advanced through the countless criss-crossing channels that he was already one of those great men. He prayed, silently, as she herself had taught him, that his father would manage to convince her.

•

Monday: 2

The French windows of the Long Room were well sealed, the flood kept resolutely at bay, and Naia just couldn't resist lying on the floor, below water level, and peering beyond the glass. There wasn't much to see, but it was an experience. Another solitary experience. Be nice to share things sometimes. Generally, though, she was more comfortable alone in this false reality. She didn't have to watch what she said when no one was listening. She knew she must eventually find a way to feel at home here, but it would have to evolve at whatever pace was necessary, unforced. Acceptance of the world that accepted her so totally would require a state of mind that she could not at present imagine.

She was still lying on the floor when the doorbell rang. Feeling caught out in a childish act, she jumped to her feet. But then she thought: the doorbell? With the water at the level it was, who, apart from the postman in his company waders, could possibly have slushed all the way to their front door – the heavily fortified door which couldn't be opened anyway?

The bell rang again. Ivan was in town and Kate was Hoovering upstairs, so it was up to her. She went out to the hall and looked through the window beside the door. A familiar figure stood where the step should be, in half a shiny black wetsuit (the bottom half).

Robert Faulkner, of all people. Her boyfriend in her true reality. Boyfriend there, virtual stranger here. She'd found that out very early on, when she'd put in a tentative call to his mobile. Same number, but the voice at the other end when she announced herself was puzzled rather than warm or pleased, clearly wondering why she was ringing him. Just one more loss to absorb, get used to.

She raised the sash. 'Yes?'

He stepped sideways in the water; stood before her. Naia's heart jumped. It was the closest she'd been to this version of him. Perhaps there could be something between them, in time. A relationship with this alternative Robert might help her adjust to the new way of things.

'You want eggs?' he said.

No special light in his eye as he looked at her. Where the other Robert couldn't keep his hands off her, this one was quite indifferent.

'Eggs?'

He indicated the high-wheeled cart he was pushing round the village. 'Fresh today. Gathered 'em meself.' His father had a smallholding, where he grew vegetables and reared a few dozen chickens.

'Did you have to dive for them?' Naia asked.

'Sorry?'

Bit slow. Serious type. Her own Robert, her lost Robert, for all his potential as a visual artist of some sort, wouldn't have gained many fans on the stand-up circuit. Ditto, this one.

'Joke,' she said. 'How's the art coming?'

He frowned. 'OK,' he said slowly, with a *What's it to you?* air.

'I heard you were going to art college in September.'

He relaxed a little. She'd touched on something close to his heart.

'Yeh. Can't wait.'

'Well...I hope it works out for you.'

'Thanks.'

After which there was little to say that was not to do with eggs. Naia went along the hall and called up to Kate several times, loudly, to make herself heard above the roar of the old vac. When she finally got a reply she returned to the window with the news.

'Sorry. Don't need any.'

'OK.' All the same to him.

She watched him push the cart away, against the resistance of the water. She might have tried harder, but she was pretty sure that nothing would have worked. There'd been no spark. None at all.

She sighed. Oh well. Closed the window.

•

Monday: 3

Father had done it! Convinced Maman to let him take the boat out – alone! How he'd managed it Aldous had no idea, nor did he ask; it was sufficient that he was going to be allowed. But there was a condition. Marie insisted on being able to see him whenever she looked out, which meant that he must not go beyond the boundaries of Withern Rise. This was a disappointment for Aldous, but Withern was a substantial property. There were a great many growing things to row around, between and under, and it was some way to any of the boundary walls. As Aldous only had Wellingtons, his father offered to carry him to the boat. They went downstairs and two steps from the water that filled the hall sat to pull their boots on. Then A.E. raised his son onto his shoulders and carried him to the porch door. The door was closed, in spite of the water being as high inside as out, but closing doors after you was a habit Marie would allow no one to break, flood or no flood.

Aldous was no lightweight, and his father struggled, but he managed to get him to the rowing boat lashed to a hook beside the River Room doors. He placed him gently in the boat and ruffled his hair. A.E. loved all four of his children, but Aldous was the one to whom he felt closest. He'd felt this since the minute the boy came into the world, when he stared at his father with large, thunder-blue eyes that seemed to say, 'Hullo, it's me!' His eye colour had shifted towards a mild blue-green as he grew older, but the bond between them had never changed. If absolutely forced to, A.E. could imagine being without his wife or his other children, even the girls, who delighted him, but life without Aldous was unthinkable. He was at least as concerned for the lad's safety as Marie, but he understood, where she did not, a growing boy's need of independence. He suppressed the cry of 'Mind how you go!' that rose to his lips, and merely waved as his beaming son set off.

Aldous rounded the corner of the house with half a dozen confident dips. His mother leant out of a window as he passed underneath. 'You be careful now, Aldous.' He laughed happily and rowed across the kitchen garden to the cemetery wall, and along the line of the wall to the side gate where, knowing he was observed from the house, he turned the boat around and followed the northern wall to the river: another point beyond which he could not go. He paused above the invisible bank, gazing longingly at the willows guarding the osier beds, then, with some regret, swung around to continue his authorised voyage through the grounds of Withern Rise.

•

Monday: 4

Alaric had got up late and taken his time over breakfast. He knew what he must do, but he wasn't looking forward to it. By eleven, having run out of excuses, he could put it off no longer. Before leaving the house, he stood in the doorway of the River Room for a minute, watching Alex working on a rag rug for her garden studio when it became usable again. It was the sort of thing Liney might have made, except that in Alex's hands it was not a scrappy hotchpotch of ill-assorted colours. Dear old Liney. He wondered what she was doing now.

Alex glanced up. 'Loose end?'

He shrugged. 'Just watching.'

'So watch from a sitting position. Talk to me.'

'I'm on my way out.'

'You'd never know it. Where are you going?'

'Just paddling around by myself.'

'You spend too much time alone these days, Alaric.'

'How much is too much?' he said.

'No idea. Something my mum used to say to me. God on a stick, I'm turning into my mother.'

'Hope I don't,' he said, and left with her chuckle in his ears.

•

Monday: 5

Shortly after eleven, in spite of her misgivings, Naia attempted the Coneygeare, inching slowly through the water hoping she wouldn't come a cropper and make a fool of herself. Every now and then she stumbled in a gully or over some unseen object, but always managed, just, not to career headlong – until she skidded on something slimy and lost her balance, sitting down with a small but undignified splash. Fortunately, the land rose a little at this point, so the water was shallower than elsewhere, but still, it was deep enough to soak her to the waist. Struggling to her feet, she found the waders half full of water, while her jeans and pants clung unpleasantly. If the ground had been dry she would have flounced home in a fury; but if the ground had been dry she wouldn't now be wet in the worst places. Cursing her stupidity for trying to cross the Coneygeare while being so certain she'd never make it, she turned and headed, with exceptional care and raised elbows, for Withern Rise.

'Nai! Nai!'

A summons from behind, across the water. Nafisa Causa and Selma Jakes waving like demented marionettes. She returned the greeting but did not turn back. Better to seem stand-offish than endure the chafing that prolonged contact with wet underwear would bring. And what did it matter, really, if these false friends were offended? Since ending up in this reality, Naia's mind had turned inward. She could never forget that she was an incomer. An impostor. These people didn't know her, they just thought they did. Only she knew the truth, that she and they were strangers. They looked and behaved and spoke like people she had known, but they were not those people. They thought they knew of her great loss when she was fourteen, but her loss was not then, it was right now, and she couldn't let on, to them or anyone. She had no doubt that as a consequence of her secret grief she wasn't doing as well in the exams as she had once expected to. She'd always been bright, clever, preferring to achieve than to fail, but an unexpected blight had eaten her life from the inside and achievement meant little now. Surrounded by clones who harked back to events and conversations in which she had not participated, it was all she could do to get through the days, to say nothing of the nights.

Monday: 6

In shorts and uncool sandals once again, Alaric started across the south garden. Nearing the Family Tree he made sure not to touch any part of it, even the raised roots below water level. The tree wasn't safe, he'd learnt that before, but he had to approach it, at least *approach* it, because last night another Alaric had dropped down from its branches, apparently realised he was in the wrong reality, and vanished. Where had he gone? Back to where he'd thought he was? And was that all it took to return you to your own reality? The realisation that you were in the wrong one?

It occurred to him that the visitor might have been the Alaric whose room he'd strayed into the snowy night in February that he'd been trying to get home from Naia's. He considered the tree. Once before it had sent him to another reality. If it could send him to one, it might be able to send him to a further one. One which contained a version of himself.

Monday: 7

Reaching the main gate, Naia started along the drive (which, she thought without humour, should be renamed 'the wade'). About to pass a gap in the shrubbery to her left, she plunged through instead, careless of what she trampled in her impatience to reach the house and dry clothes. The shortcut took her into the south garden. She was passing beneath the Family Tree when she heard a rustling overhead, followed by a tiny self-pitying mew. Moving closer to the trunk, she saw a small white shape peering down at her, wide-eyed, fearful, shivering.

'You daft mog. What are you doing up there?'

The tree was some distance from the nearest dry land, which meant the cat must have swum here. Few domestic cats enjoy water, but this one didn't seem to know that. Three times in the past two days she'd seen this bold little creature splashing around the garden, and rescued him. Today she hadn't seen him, hadn't been there to stop him, and he'd made it this far. An astonishing feat.

Emboldened by her presence, the cat began a timorous descent by a complicated route. He didn't seem his usual sassy self. Nerves, she assumed, holding her arms up to encourage him. The small animal edged gradually lower and lower, but reaching a point below which he felt unable to continue he stopped, meowed, waited for her to do something about it.

'Oh, I see,' Naia said. 'You're brave enough to swim half the garden, but a tiny little jump is too much for you.'

Wishing she could remove her water-filled boots, but aware that it would take far too much effort while actually standing in water, she began to climb. Her legs felt like lead. The cat waited for her, not taking his eyes off her for an instant.

•

Monday: 8

The old tree didn't look too fit up close, Alaric thought. The bark was discoloured here and there, and leaves which should be fresh and bright at this time of year seemed smaller and duller than usual. Perhaps having its roots under water didn't agree with it. Nor surprising if so. It wasn't a water-loving willow after all.

He waded round the back to conceal himself from the house. He took a deep breath and touched the trunk. When nothing happened he settled his palm on it, and waited. Still nothing. He took his hand away. The palm felt moist. There was a thin sticky liquid on it. Reddish brown. Blood of the tree. He dipped his hand in the water and wiped it on his shorts. His palm was still sticky. He returned it to the water, waggled it furiously, and when he withdrew it, rubbed it on another part of the bark. Better. He looked up. That great bough half a metre above his head: his favourite sitting place when he was younger. Be good to sit there again, just for a minute, with the world below so altered. He reached up; hauled himself out of the water. It wasn't as easy as it used to be. Being so much bigger and heavier now, it took some effort to get up there. But he managed it. He was just settling himself on the bough when he felt a slight quiver in the tree. Fear gripped him. He'd done the wrong thing, risked too much. He prepared to jump down. Perhaps if he was quick enough he…

Too late. The tree had changed. And he was no longer alone.

Monday: 9

She had pulled herself up to the bough from which the cat stared. He looked very feeble, not his usual sprightly self at all. Settling herself astride the bough, she held her palm out.

'Come to mother, scaredy-cat.'

The cat offered a timid forepaw, which, she saw, had been dipped in something thick and white. Looked like snow. Ridiculous, she thought as she reached for the cat. Before she could take hold of him, however, she felt a small dislocation, as if the tree had moved the merest fraction. Steadying herself, she realised that the tree was now subtly different. But what shook her most were the eyes that stared at her from along the bough. Not the cat's eyes. The cat was gone.

Monday: 10

Much as he was enjoying it, Aldous needed a break from rowing. Passing near his favourite tree he moored alongside it. The boat rocked a little as he stood up, but he steadied it against the trunk. He glanced towards the house. His mother's face was not in any of the windows. He swung up without effort and sat on the lowest bough surveying his watery domain. The tree was far older than him, but because of its name he had always thought of it as *his* tree. Aldous's Oak. He was proud of that. After a minute or two, he decided to climb higher. He felt his way upward through the dense foliage, hauling himself from bough to branch with confidence and ease. He might have gone further still if not for the sudden voices below. He returned the way he'd come, dropping silently stage by stage, until he was just above them. He made a spy-hole in the leaves. There were two of them, a boy and a girl, around seventeen, sitting on the bough some distance apart.

'You're not having it back,' the boy was saying. 'It's mine now, end of story.'

'Suits you then, does it?' the girl replied.

'Yeah, it suits me. It's the way things should've been.'

'It's the way things *were*. For *me*! You've stolen my life!'

'I've stolen nothing. I didn't plan it. It just worked out that way.'

'In your favour. Have you any idea what I've been going through? It's been hell. I live in a world of strangers, and I don't even have my mother any more. I bet she wouldn't know me if I walked in the room and sat down at the— '

Naia broke off. A rustling above their heads. She looked up. They both did. A boy's face was framed in the leaves.

'Who the *hell*?' Alaric said.

Then legs were dangling, toes feeling for the bough, on which the boy stood a moment, arms extended into the greenery above.

'Three on one branch might not be such a good idea,' Naia said.

Alaric curled his lip. 'Even two's a crowd.'

Aldous dropped to his haunches between them. 'What are you doing in my tree?'

Naia smiled. 'Your tree?'

'Yes. Mine.'

'We've been here before,' Alaric said.

Naia bent to look between the lowest branches and the water. Even a cursory glance revealed differences.

'When have we been here before?'

'I mean arguing about who owns what.' He also bent to look. 'The kid says it's his tree. His house too then.'

Aldous scowled. 'Who are you calling a kid? I might

have taken you to the gate, but I don't like being called a kid.'

'Taken us to the gate?' Alaric said. 'How? On your back?'

Aldous aimed a toe at the boat bumping the trunk below.

'Is that yours?' Naia asked.

'It is today. But I can't go far.' He thumped the tree with his heel. 'Maman says.'

'Maman?'

'My mother.'

Alaric butted in impatiently, addressing Aldous. 'Do you know anyone who looks like me?'

'Why would he?' Naia said, surprised by both question and tone.

'Another reality. Anything's possible.'

'Yes...' she said slowly, absorbing it. 'Another *reality*.'

She bent down again, peered around as well as she was able from her perch. There were more trees in this south garden. Two of them, fruit trees, supported between them a hammock made of what looked like thick brown rope, its lowest part floating on the water. From a bough of the apple tree there also dangled a short unpainted plank, a makeshift swing, half submerged.

'Are you coming or not?' Aldous said. When Alaric grunted a surly 'No,' he jumped down into the boat. 'Still my tree.'

'We won't hurt it,' Naia assured him.

'You didn't answer my question!' Alaric shouted as he rowed away.

Aldous didn't answer.

'Must be the way you asked it,' Naia said. She straightened. 'Interesting. A different Underwood at Withern Rise.'

'You don't know he's an Underwood.'

'Of course he is. Didn't you notice the shape of his head, his nose, his chin?'

'No.'

She glanced down again. 'The water's higher here.'

'So? It's an alternative reality.'

'With alternative flood conditions?' He shrugged – which made her suspicious. 'Do you know something?' He looked away. 'Have you been to other realities as well as this?'

'One other,' he admitted reluctantly.

'I don't understand,' she said. 'How? Didn't your Folly break too?'

'It broke.'

'How badly?'

'Totally.'

'So how did you get to another reality? Or to this one, come to that. How did I get here?'

'It's the tree,' he said.

'The tree?'

'It has...properties.'

'What sort of properties?'

'That's all I know. That boy...'

'What about him?'

'If he's an Underwood his parents must be here too. They might be an alternative Alex and Ivan.'

'Impossible. Different child.'

'Maybe they had another kid here.'

'What, instead of one of us?'

'As well as.'

She considered this. 'We ought to check it out.'

'How?'

'By getting down from this tree, for a start.'

'Feel free.'

'You'll come, won't you?'

'You're the one with the boots. Are they Grandpa Rayner's?'

'Yes. And they're full of water. Weigh a ton.'

'How come?'

'I fell over crossing the Coneygeare.'

He laughed. 'Clumsy git.'

Another time she might have seen the funny side

too, but his derision reminded her of all that she'd lost. And who in particular.

'How is she?'

'Who?' he said blandly.

'Who'd you think? Is she well? Does she ever...you know.'

'Talk about you? When she has no idea you ever existed?'

Hearing it so pitilessly put, Naia wilted. Alaric closed his mind to her misery. She was the true heir to all that he'd come to think of as his, and she was dangerously near. The danger, if past experience was anything to go by, was that a single touch between them might return him to his old reality, old life. What he didn't know, because she was careful not to give it away, was that his heartlessness had nudged her thoughts along similar lines.

'Looks brighter,' she said, leaning forward and down to peer past him.

'What does?'

'The house, the brickwork, all of it. Fresher.'

He bent down to see for himself.

'Shutters at the windows too,' she added, inching closer while he looked the other way. 'I think my Withern once had shutters and the ivy isn't as widely spread or as thick. And look, over there, a sort of summerhouse. We haven't got a— '

It was only his wariness of her that caused him to look round. When his head started to turn Naia flung her hand out, intending to touch him while she could. He saw it coming, yelled, jumped out of reach just in time, but in dodging lost his balance and fell from the tree, into the water. And when he spluttered to the surface...

'Oh, very clever. You can drown in two inches of water, I tell him, and what does he say? Leave off, he says, I'm nearly seventeen. Well I hate to point it out, Alaric, but this is even more than two inches.'

He sat up, in water that fell just below his chest. Alex, in Grandpa Rayner's old waders, gazed down at him with amusement. He looked about him.

The extra trees were gone. So were the shutters. Naia.

Monday: 11

Almost every day there was a new memory waiting for him when he woke. A gift of the morning. During the past few months Aldous had recalled such a quantity of unsorted fragments that he wondered how many more there were to be recaptured. They were mostly undramatic memories, but few were unpleasant. His uncomfortable sleeping arrangements were easier to bear for the thought of what the next waking might bring.

Last night, settling down, he thought again of his gran. She often came into his mind at night, like a radiant guest. She was the rock of his life. If some of the others were still a little hazy, she was not. He imagined that she'd cared for the other children as much as for him, but as yet he had no memory of her cuddling them, reading to them, bathing them. It pleased him to think that he was her favourite.

Occasionally a less welcome memory returned, such as an incident during a visit from the Montagniers – Uncle Mathieu and Aunt Eléne – who'd come from Limoges to spend Easter with them. Uncle Mathieu was one of those adults who adopt a superior air when talking to children, as if their own age, being greater, elevates them above the young. Aldous could only recall meeting him and his wife once before that visit. They had not been drawn to one another. Aldous's coolness became active dislike during the afternoon of Easter Monday when the adults were gathered round the draw-leaf table in the Long Room. Maman – his uncle's younger sister – had made a large pot of tea, and there were scones with home-made jam, and neat little egg-and-cress and cucumber sandwiches with the crusts trimmed off. 'Oh, how very *English*!' Tante Eléne had exclaimed dismissively. Aldous, Ursula and Mimi were given bread and dripping, while Ray, the youngest, received Marmite, his favourite. For some reason, Gran was absent that weekend. Her warmth, her natural gaiety, were sorely missed – by him anyway. Father struggled to keep things light, no easy task in such lofty company. The incident that had embedded itself so deeply in Aldous's mind occurred when he dropped his spoon on the floor and wanted a clean one to stir his tea with. He started towards the table, where the cutlery lay on a silver tray.

'Borrow mine, young man,' said Uncle Mathieu.

'No thank you. I want my own.'

He reached past for one of the unused teaspoons on the tray, but before his fingers could close on it Uncle Mathieu inserted his arm in the space between boy and spoon. He spoke through his teeth, which, Aldous noticed, resembled a double row of mossy tombstones.

'I said…use *mine*.'

His uncle's eyes were very cold beneath eyebrows like grey wire. There was a crumb lodged in his moustache.

'I'd like a clean one,' Aldous said.

Mathieu held his spoon upright like a small trophy. Tea dribbled down the handle, onto his nicotine-stained fingers.

'Take mine or do without.'

For Aldous it was a moment of decision. It would have been easier to accept the spoon, but he didn't want his uncle's spoon, or anyone else's, he wanted his own. He bit his lip and spun about; marched the length of the room, which had fallen silent. He went out to the hall, and upstairs to the galleried landing and his bedroom, hoping no one had realised how close he'd been to tears. Gran would have known. Gran wouldn't have let his uncle bully him. He needed her that day. He really needed her.

But she wasn't there.

Monday: 12

Naia did not remain long after Alaric's fall. She had no choice in this, for at the instant he hit the water the bough shifted under her and she was in her version of the tree. Returned with so little ceremony to her point of departure, she was startled when her cat snuggled into her arms. It was all she could do to both hold on to him and retain her balance, for she was suddenly overcome with exhaustion, as though she'd exerted herself more than was good for her. Cradling the cat in one arm, she lowered herself into the water and forced her weary legs towards the house. She dropped him through the window and climbed after him. Inside, she wanted only to sink to the carpet and rest, but she managed to remove her boots on an old sheet thoughtfully provided by Kate, tip the water out (of the window) and go upstairs. In the bathroom, she splashed cold water on her face, which revived her a little before going to her room to change out of her wet things.

Similarly drained, it took every ounce of Alaric's strength to dry himself and put on some fresh clothes. But half an hour after their return, he and Naia sat in armchairs in their respective Long Rooms. They had some thinking to do. Neither of them welcomed the intrusion when Alex and Kate came in.

'You all right?' one asked.

'Look a bit peaky,' said the other.

Two replies, identical: 'Overdid it out there,' and without further discussion they were left alone. Kate Faraday and Alex Underwood were more alike than anyone knew. Anyone but Naia.

Monday: 13

The discovery of two strangers in his tree hadn't concerned Aldous much. He was rowing around the garden: much more interesting. Venturing some little way into the Coneygeare, he was suddenly overcome by guilt and rowed back to the garden. He paused under the oak to see if the visitors were still there. They weren't, so he rowed round the house, to the mooring point. He hadn't thought how he would get indoors, but his father, just returning from checking the tomatoes in the flooded greenhouse, carried him in.

Maman was sitting on the lower stairs, awaiting her wandering son's return, though she did not say as much. A.E. passed him up. 'Mind your feet,' Marie said to Aldous. 'Not that it matters, the carpet's *quite* ruined.'

She sat him beside her to tug his boots off, wet from a few inches of water in the boat, and was lodging them between banister rails to dry when pandemonium broke out above: Ursula chasing her young sister and brother along the landing accompanied by Mimi's high-pitched screams and little Ray's croaky roar of terror. Their mother stormed upstairs to impose order, but at the top changed her mind, largely because by this time she was alone there. The two youngest had charged into the box room and Ursula, shoving against the door with her shoulder, had just managed to squeeze inside. The mayhem continued – cries, squeals, laughter, thuds – but sufficiently subdued by the sturdy door for Marie to decide to leave them to it.

Aldous, on the lower stairs, noticed that his mother's face was grey with strain. She'd been stuck indoors for days, unable to shop, talk to neighbours, even get to her kitchen and prepare proper meals. Marie felt that she was letting her family down by not providing adequate fare, refusing to believe that the children were happy with scraps – or, indeed, that her husband was relieved not to have to eat so well. The combination of early middle-age and his wife's cooking wasn't doing A.E.'s waistline much good at all, and he didn't care for the extra chin that was beginning to swell below the original. But here was a man as pleased with life as he felt anyone had a right to be. With a flourishing business, a fine house, an attractive (if rather too thin) French wife, and children he doted on, he could not imagine being more contented with his lot. If told by a clairvoyant, he would have dismissed any idea that in a matter of days disaster would strike, contentment end.

Monday: 14

Trudging across the mass of swallowed land known these days as Withy Meadows, Aldous wished his legs were as young as his mind said they were. After attending to his ablutions at the toilet block in the car park, he climbed the steps to the town bridge. Others had congregated on the bridge, for the novelty of standing on dry ground. Jocular remarks were exchanged, but Aldous avoided all conversation.

Passing down the bridge he reached the High Street and an enormous swimming pool dotted with tall lamps: the market square. He was about to cross the square when a name came to him that he doubted he'd thought of for six full decades, awake or asleep. Eric Hobb. He stopped in his tracks. Eric Hobb! Where had that come from? He cast about him, and saw:

HOBB, MORRIS AND GECK

FAMILY SOLICITORS & NOTARIES
Serving the community

Then it unfolded in his mind. Eric's story. The whole sad business.

Eric was fifteen when he was nine, which meant that they had little to do with one another. Different generations then. Eric lived with his mother and twelve-year-old sister at 42 Main Street, Eynesford, two doors down from the butcher's. Everyone knew Eric Hobb. Eric and his bike. Eric loved his bike. It could whisk him in and out of slow traffic, get him from here to there in no time. He was in such command of his vehicle that it was a surprise as well as a shock when the accident occurred.

It was the weekend, a Saturday, and Eric had set out for the bicycle shop in Stone. The bike shop was his favourite place on earth, he always said. He didn't buy much there, but he liked to look and touch, and the owner, Terry Eagle, a fellow enthusiast in his thirties, was always happy to talk about bikes. The market town of Stone began on the far side of the little humpback bridge above the woodyard estuary. The boundary was marked by a modest seventeenth century coaching inn known as The Sorry Fiddler, which stood at the corner where the road swept both ways around St Cecilia's churchyard. A small car park lay beyond a brick archway attached to the pub, but cars were fewer then, and in any case The Fiddler was a short walk from both village and town. The only car there the day of the accident was the 1938 Ford Sedan belonging to Bill Ockham, mobile representative of a firm of razor manufacturers. Mr Ockham had popped in for a pint of best in the middle of the day. While there, he also consumed a portion of Woolton Pie and smoked a Craven 'A' while eyeing the effervescent thirty-six-year-old barmaid's hand-knitted chest.

While Eric Hobb was pausing on the bridge to peer over the wall at the pine logs jostling one another below, Mr Ockham was climbing into his car with the intention of driving the three or four miles to Eaton Fane and continuing his rounds. As the razor salesman put his car into gear and lowered his foot on the accelerator, Eric stood up on his pedals and launched himself down the steep slope of the bridge. The road was clear, but as he was about to sweep past the pub the Ford shot through the archway. He and his bike went under the car. The bike was buckled, but not beyond repair. Eric's skull was shattered, his life extinguished in the wink of an eye.

Aldous did not speculate as to how the accident might have been avoided, but it was a simple matter. If Eric had not paused on the bridge there would have been no fatality. Because he started down when he did, several other lives were also changed, not least that of Helen Stoker, the girl he would have married seven years on, and the two children they would have produced. Mr Ockham and Eric's mother were the most obvious casualties. The razor salesman suffered such torment for the life he'd taken that, eighteen months later, he posted farewell gifts to his three young grandchildren before slitting his wrists in another pub car park, with one of his own sample products. The effect of the accident on Eric's mother was more long-term, but no less tragic. Her husband, Bruce, had left her eight years earlier for one of the younger female staff at Stone Library, since when he had contributed little to their children's upkeep and provided nothing at all for her. She worked as a counter assistant at the Co-op: small wages to cover the rent and support two children. Life was already far from good for Geraldine Hobb when her eldest died. His death was the final blow. It did not drive her to drink (which she couldn't have afforded anyway) or to suicide, but into a long decline laden with misery, negativity and regret that lasted until her eighty-sixth year.

'Morning, Aldous,' said a voice.

Aldous Underwood turned. 'Hullo, Mr Knight.'

These two had first met a couple of weeks after Aldous's return in February. Being dedicated strollers, their paths had often crossed since then. Sometimes when they met they continued on together, even if they had not previously been going in the same direction. They even walked in these flood conditions, though only Mr Knight was suitably attired. Aldous's trouser legs were soaked through, but it didn't bother him overmuch. He was just glad to be here with all his senses. When introducing themselves at their second meeting, Aldous had provided his full name, which for some reason seemed to surprise Mr Knight, who had merely said 'Knight' when proffering his hand. This was fine with Aldous. He would have felt odd calling his new acquaintance by his first name. To him, if only to him, Mr Knight was very much his senior. At some point, previously, Mr Knight had told him that his father was gardener at Withern Rise in the thirties and forties. Hearing this, Aldous's memory of the father was jogged. He and the present Mr Knight talked of many things during their encounters, but it was Aldous who offered the most about himself. It was good to tell someone. This morning, however, he didn't really want to talk. He couldn't have said why. Mr Knight was his usual self: friendly, but not verbose. To fill a gap as they stood not really passing the time of day beside the flooded market square, Aldous indicated the sign that had released the latest memory.

'I used to know a Hobb,' he said.

'That's Johnny Hobb,' Mr Knight told him. 'Eric's son.'

'Eric? My Hobb was an Eric. But he died as a lad. Accident.'

'Well this one's still about. Still riding his bike in his late seventies. Quite a character.'

Aldous glanced about him. An electricity showroom occupied the premises next to Woolworth's. Yesterday, when he'd looked in the window, it was a greetings-card shop. He'd done it again. Crossed over without noticing. Eric Hobb was still alive here. An old man. Here, he hadn't paused on the bridge.

•

Monday: 15

Evening. Naia sat in her room, pampered cat in lap, thinking about the other reality. That Withern Rise looked rather nice, she thought. Bit old-fashioned, but cosy. She'd noticed a small tin hut standing in the water near the kitchen, roof covered in turf. What could that be? A playhouse for young children? And the boy in the tree. Obviously an Underwood. She leant back, not forgetting to stroke the cat. She'd spoken to an Underwood who had never existed for her until that morning. It was like the first time Alaric turned up. No idea about him till then. She wondered about the boy's family. Parents called Alex and Ivan as Alaric had suggested? Or another Kate instead of Alex perhaps? And suppose he had an older sister. A sister called Naia. She put herself in such a Naia's position. A brother. Someone to talk to, tell all this to, trust not to pass it on. She rolled her eyes. A kid brother would probably have to be bribed into silence. Still. Even with several years between them, even here, she wouldn't be as lonely with a brother.

Her thoughts turned to Alaric's presence in the tree. It must have been their simultaneous act of climbing their separate family trees that had brought them together in the third one at a Withern Rise unfamiliar to them both.

She wondered if it could happen again, and if she and Alaric had to be in the tree at the same time for them to be transported to this new reality. Pity if so. She would like to go back there, but she wasn't sure she wanted to see him again. She'd forgotten that he wasn't the greatest company in the world. Any world.

Monday: 16

From his bedroom window, Alaric gazed across at the Family Tree. He too was thinking about the other reality. He couldn't shake the idea that there might be another Alaric there. How strange, he thought, to talk to a version of yourself whose life was identical to yours in every way. Well, there might be the odd difference. Another Alaric might have a different haircut, like to go fishing, be top of his class (or bottom), have a girlfriend. A girlfriend could be interesting. If Alaric 2 had a girlfriend, he, Alaric 1, might have seen a version of her. She might have given him the eye and he hadn't noticed, or been too shy to follow things up.

He thought of Naia. It had probably been a fluke that she was there the same time as him. She might not be another time. But then again she might. And next time she might succeed in touching him. One touch and he could be back where he came from, motherless once more, Kate Faraday running things, everything so tatty, nothing much to live for, look forward to.

In spite of the threat posed by contact with Naia, he was tempted to try a return visit to the new reality. But only tempted. He retreated from the window. Sleep on it. See how he felt in the morning.

TUESDAY

Tuesday: 1

Aldous had asked his mother if he could go a little further today, but she remained adamant. After completing two circuits of the garden, beginning to grow bored, he again found himself near the tree, which reminded him of yesterday's visitors. Pulling closer, he called softly. 'Hullo? You there?' He would have been surprised if they'd been up there again, but the lack of a reply told him what he needed to know: that he had his tree to himself, the way he liked it.

He stood up in the boat and set his back against the trunk. He could see most of the property from there, apart from the north garden. Born in the house, like his father, like Ursula and Ray but not Mimi, he had seen his first sights within those boundary walls. The sense of enclosure suited him. For half his life the world outside had been an arena of conflict which had intruded hardly at all on Withern Rise. He could barely remember a time when the wireless was not ritually tuned in for the seven o'clock news, when silence was expected as the sombre newsreader with the superior voice reported the latest casualties, triumphs, patriotic declarations. He'd never paid much attention to the news. Nor had Mimi and Ray. Only Ursula had listened, latterly at least. From the age of eight she had taken to standing close to Father when the news was on, leaning forward with him to catch every nuance of the sonorous tones issuing from the speaker. When the main bulletin was over she would give a small nod, as if to say that she understood all she'd heard, before returning to the equally important business of childhood.

The nearest Withern had come to being touched by the conflict was the German Heinkel that came down in the Coneygeare in the spring of 1941. Engine failure, Father said. A bunch of lads had been first on the scene. There was a rumour that the pilot was still alive then, just about, and that Jed Cronyn had punched him in the mouth and pulled one of his teeth as a souvenir. The only thing anyone knew for certain was that the pilot was dead by the time the police arrived. The broken body was taken away and kids and adults from all about converged on what was left of the strange foreign aircraft, pinching anything that was loose or could be easily removed: trophies to be gazed upon years afterwards with the pride of warriors who had risked all.

'It worked, then.'

Aldous started. A voice from above.

'Just climbed up, had you?'

Two voices.

'Yeh. Wanted to see if it would happen again.'

'Great minds.'

'Don't flatter yourself.'

'It is the same reality, isn't it?'

'If it isn't, the kid's got a double in some other.'

Naia leaned down. 'Hi.'

'Pardon?' said Aldous.

'Are you planning on pulling that stunt again?' Alaric asked her.

'What stunt?'

'You know bloody well.'

'No, don't worry.'

'How do I know?'

'Because I'm *telling* you. When I give my word I keep it.'

'Don't mind me, will you?' Aldous said.

'We're having a private conversation here,' Alaric informed him.

'In my tree.'

'What do you want – rent?'

'Don't mind him, he's a misery,' Naia said to Aldous.

Aldous groped in his pocket; raised a paper bag aloft.

'Who'd like an aniseed ball?'

Naia shook her head for both of them and asked his name. When he told her she could not respond immediately.

'Why the surprise?' Alaric said. 'It was you said he was an Underwood.'

'It's not that…'

'Why don't you come down?' Aldous asked then.

'And do what?' Alaric said. 'Pootle around in your piddling little boat?'

'It's a nice boat. My dad made it.'

'Oh yes? Flatpack, was it?'

'Sorry?'

'Have you got a brother?'

'Yes… Why?'

'I knew it!'

Naia returned to the conversation. Disappointedly. 'I thought you might have a sister.'

'I have. Two of them.'

'Two? You have two sisters?'

'Yes. Ursula and Mimi.'

'Ursula and...?'

'Mimi.'

Alaric leant down, eagerly. 'What's your brother's name?'

'Ray.'

The eagerness withered. 'Ray?'

'What are your parents called?' Naia asked.

Aldous frowned. 'Why are you asking all these questions?'

'Just curious.'

'Curiosity killed the cat.'

'It'll certainly do for mine if he doesn't watch out,' she said. 'Their names aren't Alex and Ivan, are they?'

'Who?'

'Your parents.'

'No.' Suddenly tight-lipped.

'Well that's cleared *that* up,' Alaric muttered.

She glanced at him. 'Have you got a family tree?'

'You know I have. How d'you think I got here?'

'I mean the one Mum put together for the back of the photo album.'

'My mother didn't get that far with hers,' he reminded her.

'What have you done with it? Your album.'

'I had to hide it. What did you do with yours?'

'It's still about, minus a few pages.'

87

'Did you chuck 'em?'

'No. I couldn't. They're in a folder under my bed.'

'And no one ever looks there?'

'Kate and I have an understanding. My room's private. No one comes in without my say-so. The drag is I have to clean and tidy it myself.'

'Why don't you just carry on as if I wasn't here?' Aldous said.

Alaric glanced down. 'We were.'

'Aldous? Aldous, what are you doing over there?'

A raised voice, woman's voice, slightly accented, from the house.

'Just talking!' Aldous shouted back.

'To the tree?'

'No, to—'

'Don't mention us!' Naia hissed.

'—myself.'

'All right. But be careful.'

'I am being careful.'

'Well continue to be.'

'Your mother?' Naia said as Marie retreated from the window. Aldous nodded. 'She sounds foreign.'

'She's French.'

'Oh, so you're half French.'

He shrugged.

'Do you speak it?'

'*Je parle autant que j'ai besoin autour ici.*'

'Is that a yes or a no?' said Alaric.

'You must need a house that size with all those brothers and sisters,' Naia said.

'One brother,' Aldous said.

'But two sisters and your parents. Six in all.'

'Seven.'

'Seven?'

'Including my Aunt Larissa. Eight when her friend Vita comes to stay. I don't like Vita. She smokes all the time.'

'Why's your aunt living with you?' Alaric asked.

'Nowhere else to go.' He sat down abruptly in the boat. 'Be seeing you.'

And he was off.

'Question,' Alaric said as Aldous rowed away.

'Yes?'

'If these are Underwoods, why are they so different?'

'I need a sight of the family tree before answering that,' Naia said.

'What will that tell you?'

'Remains to be seen.'

'Why don't you just tell me what you're thinking?'

'And be sneered at if I'm wrong? No thanks.'

The tree moved very slightly about them.

'What's that?' Alaric said nervously.

Naia had little doubt; became efficient. 'Come back tomorrow, ten o'clock.'

'Come back?'

'Climb your tree at ten in the mor—'

She was gone. So was he. Each to their own point of departure, where their strength was instantly drained from them. It took everything they had to get to the house.

Tuesday: 2

This was the morning Mr Knight brought Aldous the boots. 'I had to guess your size,' he said. 'Hope they fit because they were the last ones in the shop. There's been quite a run on them.'

'They're for me?' Aldous said.

'Yes. Try them.'

It would have been an odd vignette to the casual observer. One man, wearing thigh boots, standing deep in water, offering a pair to another, sitting in a hammock. Mr Knight steadied the hammock while Aldous pulled one of the boots on.

'Stiff,' he said when his leg was covered.

'You'll need to break them in. Wiggle your toes.'

Aldous wiggled his toes. 'Plenty of room.'

'Not too much?'

'Just enough.'

'Try the other one.'

He pulled the second wader on. His legs stuck out stiffly before him. 'You sure they'll bend?'

'A few days' use should do it.'

Aldous began to struggle down from the hammock. Mr Knight gripped his arm to help him.

'I can manage.'

'Sure you can.'

Then Aldous was in the water, stiff-legged in his tall green boots, at which they both gazed as if expecting them to dance.

'Sure they're not too tight?' Mr Knight said.

'Seem all right.'

'Because I can't take them back once you've walked about in them.'

'No, no. They're good.'

'Walk up and down then.'

Aldous walked up and down a few times. 'Feel like a scarecrow.'

'I've been meaning to talk to you about that,' Mr Knight said.

'Eh?'

'I thought we might pop down to the Sue Ryder shop.'

'The charity shop?'

'Charity's when you get something for nothing. They sell things there. Like clothing.'

'I don't need any clothing,' Aldous said.

'That coat's seen better days.'

'Not surprising. I got it off a tramp.'

'A tramp?'

'He had two and I was cold, so he gave one to me.'

'Decent of him.'

'I didn't ask for it.'

'I'm sure you didn't.'

'And I'm not asking now. This coat's fine.'

'Let's talk about it over breakfast,' Mr Knight said.

'What breakfast?'

'I thought we might wade into town and have a little something at a caff to toast your dry legs.'

'I like toast,' Aldous said.

'So do I. But we could have bacon, too. And eggs, sausages, tomatoes.'

Aldous's stomach gurgled. But he was suspicious. No one had ever bought him breakfast before. Not that he could remember.

'What's this all about? Boots, coats, breakfast. It's not my birthday.'

'When is your birthday?'

'I don't remember.'

'So let's call it your birthday.'

Aldous's reserve crumbled. The word 'birthday' warmed him. He might not remember the date of his, but he remembered the last time it had been celebrated. It was his eleventh, and the first and last that Aunt Larissa had given him something. Larissa and birthdays; standing joke:

'Nothing from Larissa.'

'Wouldn't feel right if there was.'

It wasn't just *his* birthday his aunt overlooked, it was everyone's. She even forgot her brother's. Forgot or ignored. But that year, no doubt because she was staying with them and had been frequently reminded, she had something for Aldous. 'They're not new,' she said, handing him the small pair of brass binoculars, unwrapped. 'Weren't new when I bought them. But they've been with me over twenty years. The things I've seen through *them* in my travels!'

The birthday commemorated by Aunt Larissa had, of course, been held at Withern Rise. Her snooty friend Vita had been there too, with her long nose and her big hats and her cigarettes. Vita was older than Larissa, some sort of writer who apparently owned a castle in Kent. Vita claimed to know about gardens, and was rather dismissive about the work that had been done at Withern Rise, to Maman's extreme, if veiled, annoyance. But there'd been jelly and blancmange and butterfly cakes, which were much more interesting to Aldous and the other children than the unwelcome visitor. Ursula baked a large gingerbread man with 'Aldous' on the chest, which made everyone laugh.

'What's so funny?' Mr Knight asked him.

'Just something I thought of.'

They went off together, keeping well away from the river bank in case they misjudged its position. Aldous walked as if his legs were made of wood, but he enjoyed their dryness.

The engulfed village was silent and deserted as they waded along Main Street, over the former woodyard bridge, past the pub where Eric Hobb died, and into Stone. Soon they were leaning through the brown waters of the market square and climbing the stairs to the dry room of the Baker's Oven beside the Cross Keys. They ordered their two breakfasts, but within five minutes Aldous became agitated, cowering, as if expecting the walls and ceiling to close in on him. He wolfed his food and shot downstairs and outside as soon as he could.

Tuesday: 3

When she'd recovered her strength, Naia returned to the Long Room for the photo album. Although she'd taken out the last few pages after her arrival in February, she hadn't removed the family tree from inside the back cover. She hadn't had the heart. Her mother had put so much into researching it and drawing it. The fact that the Alex of this reality hadn't lived long enough to complete the work was sad, but the only person who might be taken aback to see the family tree in its finished form was Ivan. She had little doubt that this Ivan would be as uninterested in a family tree as her real father had been the whole time her mother was working on it – even though the family in question was his rather than hers. Dad's interest in his forebears had been close to zero.

To Naia's surprise, the album wasn't in its usual place next to the old set of *Encyclopaedia Britannicas*. She asked Kate if she'd seen it.

'I saw Ivan with it a week or so ago,' Kate told her. 'But I don't know where he put it. You could ring him at the shop...'

Ivan had gone to check that his fortifications were still holding against the floodwater. In her old reality Naia wouldn't have had any hesitation in ringing him, at the shop or anywhere else, but it was different here. While she could do the father-daughter charade to his face, she had not so far been able to phone him, on any pretext. She didn't phone him now either, but, unable to summon the patience to bide her time until he returned, she went upstairs to look through the late Alex's papers.

She'd discovered the suitcase in the box room a few weeks ago, under some rubbish Ivan had chucked in because he didn't know what else to do with it. It contained most of the things to be found in an identical suitcase in Naia's birth-reality, including a certain magazine article, obituary and drawing. She found what she was looking for in an A4 buff envelope that she hadn't opened previously, but there her luck ended. Alaric's mother had died before she'd had a chance to gather all the information that Naia's mother had continued to assemble after the accident and finally, last Autumn, transform into the Underwood family tree. The notes, diagrams and unassigned dates made little sense to Naia, which meant that she had to wait for Ivan after all. Frustrating, when she was so keen to see if her suspicions were justified or just plain mad.

Tuesday: 4

'Boat-house' was a rather grandiose term for the little hut tucked into the river bank some metres along from the landing stage. Many years ago, Eldon Underwood, Alaric's great-great-grandfather, had cut a hollow in the bank to accommodate a wooden shelter for the little boat he took out when he wanted to be alone. According to Elizabeth Arnott Underwood, his biographer and unmet granddaughter-in-law, Eldon had written most of his post-1914 poetry in that boat.* By the early years of the twenty-first century, however, the boat-house was forgotten, overgrown, virtually impossible to pick out even from across the river, especially in summer when the dense foliage of an enormous willow fell across it. The boat had rotted away years ago.

Alaric had discovered the boat-house when he was ten. He'd been splashing about in the river and had swum into it before he realised what it was. Exploring the interior he found, just under the roof, the dry ledge Eldon had used for storing his works-in-progress. In the autumn of 1939, aware that death was close, Eldon had removed all his papers, so Alaric found nothing but a few dead insects, a ball of garden twine, and a knife. The latter was a large jack-knife, with a single blade which folded into a long, rather discoloured bone handle. Not much of a thing in his eyes: he had a better knife of his own, and newer. So he left it with the dead insects and the twine. But he'd never forgotten that secret hidey-hole, and last March, needing somewhere to conceal the family album, he sought and found an

*Collections by E.C. Underwood: *The Rags of War* (1898), *Hunting Mallarmé* (1916), *A Grief Rekindled* (1925), *Withies* (1941, posthumous)

identical boat-house in this reality. Here, too, there was a recessed shelf containing a ball of twine and a long folding knife. Again he left the twine, but this time he pocketed the knife. A memento.

Having decided where to hide the album he'd needed something to wrap it in, keep it dry, and had found a heavy-duty polythene bag, rather like a small sack, in the cupboard under the stairs. Large enough to enclose the book with room to spare, the bag had a long, looped drawstring of some industrial-strength cord which, pulled taut and wound round, secured and waterproofed it. He lodged the package in the boat-house, well back on the ledge, confident that it would never be found.

But now, three months on, he wanted to retrieve it. Naia's curious remarks about the family tree in her album had turned his mind to his own album. There was no family tree in his, but suddenly he needed to hold the book again, leaf through his previous life.

He waited until evening, when Alex and Ivan were watching TV. To get down to the boat-house he had to fight his way through the fringe of willow leaves overhanging the bank, to four badly eroded concrete steps. Ordinarily the top three steps would be dry, but all of them were under water now and he descended with great care. At the bottom he had to crouch and step sideways into the hut, which was more than half full of water and smelt rather unpleasant. It was dark inside, but groping under the roof he found what he'd come for. The polythene was perfectly dry.

Gaining the bank once more, he lingered behind the willow's veil while he made as sure as he could that he was not being observed from the house. About to break out, he sensed something nearby. Turning, seeing nothing untoward, he remembered Grandpa Rayner bringing him here. Grandpa had said that when you stepped well under the willow, near the trunk, the world seemed to withdraw a little. Alaric had tried it at his grandfather's bidding, and it was true. Even natural sounds seemed to diminish near the trunk. The place was strange also in that it was the only bit of the garden where nothing grew, even wild grass and weeds. Grandpa had told him that when he was a young lad, in summer, he used to hide in there, waiting for someone at the house to miss him. The willow was nothing like its present size then, but it had provided enough cover for his small squatting frame.

'I would try and find worms and snails and bugs here,' Rayner had said. 'But there were none, ever. It was as if the ground would allow nothing to live in it, or on it. Didn't seem to mind me being here, though. And you know, sometimes...'

'Sometimes what?'

'I heard voices.'

'Voices?'

'Not-quite-there voices. Other sounds, too, which shouldn't have been here.'

'Weren't you scared?'

'Oh, it wasn't frightening. I enjoyed the oddness. It was my secret place. And now it's yours.'

Alaric hadn't said as much, but to him it was just a patch of dead earth. He went there once after Rayner died, to see if he could hear those not-quite-there voices and sounds of his, but there was nothing, and he'd never returned. This time, too, he heard nothing. That mildly disconcerting feeling of something elusive, intangible, that was all.

He returned to the house as speedily as the floodwater would allow. Climbing in the window beside the porch door, he kicked his sandals off and ran up to his room. He was about to unwrap the album when Alex called him from the bottom of the stairs. He put it in his wardrobe, right at the back, to look at later. When later came, he decided it could wait until morning. In the morning he overslept, and forgot about it

Part Two
COMPETING WITH MASKS

WEDNESDAY

Wednesday: 1

Ivan denied all knowledge of the album's whereabouts.

'What do you mean?' Naia said. 'You must know where it is. Kate saw you with it.'

'Did she? Well, if I had it I don't know where I put it. What do you want it for anyway?'

'Just to look at. I'm entitled, aren't I?'

'If I come across it you'll be the first to know.'

'Oh, thanks. Much appreciated, I'm sure.'

That was last night. She spent the rest of the evening searching for it, to no avail. The one time she needed it and it was nowhere to be found.

This morning, still annoyed, she left the house ten minutes before she needed to, intending to vent some spleen by splashing around the garden. Climbing out of the window in still-damp waders, she was startled to see someone walking away from the waterlogged Family Tree and plunging through the bushes to the drive. It was the old man from the cemetery; the one she'd met the first day of her exile who had given his name as Aldous Underwood. Another Aldous! Then, too, that first dreadful day, the name had taken her by surprise, for three days earlier she had found a curious letter, signed 'Aldous U, Withern Rise', in the Family Tree of her rightful reality. Since her sole encounter with the man, she'd seen him just three times, always in the distance, once leaning on the long river bridge, once strolling through the village with Mr Knight, and yesterday in the lane between the cemetery and her old school. But now he'd come into the garden, actually come into the *garden*, and presumably been to the Family Tree. Why? For what reason? Could it be…?

She had already persuaded herself that it was a variation of this man who had placed the letter in the message hole of her original Family Tree. The two realities were the same in most details, but things sometimes happened at different times. Mr Knight had proved this by turning up to offer his help in the present garden some time after his double had offered his services in her previous one. So. Perhaps the man who called himself Aldous Underwood had just placed a letter in the message hole of this Family Tree – four months after his doppelganger had placed the same letter in the other.

Reaching the tree, Naia peered into the hole. It was dark in there, but when she reached in to feel below the lip she touched something. She lifted out an envelope crudely made of some sort of fabric that appeared to have been treated with oil or wax, probably to make it waterproof. It was very similar, if not identical, to the one she'd found – and left behind – in her old reality. It even bore the same inscription, 'To the Finder', and, like the other, was sealed with red wax impressed with the letter 'A'.

Much as she wanted to check that the envelope contained the same document, she decided to leave it for later, when she could study it at her leisure, in her room. Rather than risk it falling out of her coat, she returned it to the hole, and started climbing.

Wednesday: 2

For much of her incarceration at Withern Rise, Larissa May Underwood, an inveterate traveller, had not been in the grandest of tempers. Strait-jackets did that to her, she said. Her brother was openly amused by her determinedly sour expression, but he was one of the few people who could get away with laughing at her to her face. To three of the children – Aldous, Ursula and little Ray – Larissa was a formidable old bird. Only Mimi actually enjoyed her company. Mimi the dreamer, who loved to read her grandfather's poetry aloud, even when she didn't understand a word, and since the age of six had been infatuated with Rupert Brooke, or his photograph. She and her aunt were often seen together, not saying much, doing less, but at ease with one another in spite of the difference in their ages.

Amused, in her way, by Aldous's recent activities in the garden, Larissa had proposed a two-person boat trip along the river. When she heard of this, Mimi begged to accompany them. Larissa had no objection, but now felt obliged to invite Ursula too. Ursula shook her head, preferring to continue her struggle with Virginia Woolf. Larissa laughed at this, actually laughed, and dropped *Orlando* back in her niece's lap. There was no suggestion that little Ray should join the outing. Marie was concerned enough when she heard that Aldous and Mimi wanted to go.

'Oh, I don't know. Suppose something should happen?'

'Suppose nothing *ever* happened?' Larissa countered grimly.

Marie backed down. She usually did with Larissa, far more readily than with anyone else. She had hardly known her sister-in-law before she came to stay eighteen months ago, and had never ceased to be wary of her; never quite warmed to her. The feeling was mutual, though both women managed to be civil most of the time, and occasionally, when they tried really hard, moderately cordial.

Aldous and his father were the only ones who had ventured out since the rising of the river. Aldous didn't mind getting his legs wet, but A.E., preferring not to, would carry his waders down to the lowest dry stair and put them on before stepping into the hall. Yesterday, however, he had fixed a long ladder to the window sill of the spare bedroom, a means of exit approved of by Larissa, who considered it 'a touch more adventurous than simply going downstairs'. She used the ladder now, followed by Mimi and Aldous, to descend to the boat her brother had brought round from its mooring place outside the River Room.

It was Larissa herself, ignoring the anxious Marie at the window, who rowed them away from the house. Aldous pretended not to see his mother either, but Mimi, all grins, waved until they slid behind the willow which overhung her late grandfather's tiny boat-house.

They could have rowed through the osier beds, or to the village, or just about anywhere else they fancied, but Larissa had decided that they would head for the town bridge, and the only way to get there was to follow the course of the river. Enormous lily pads, chained to the river bed by long, supple stalks, lurked below the surface, but a few, pushing upward, ornamented the way. Mimi delighted in dipping a hand in the water and tracing the outline of the lilies in passing, and once risked falling in by leaning out to pluck one of the yellow crowns which, for the rest of the journey, she wore in her hair.

As Larissa rowed – with a verve the children had never seen in her before – she became almost garrulous, telling them things about herself that they had not been privy to before. Larissa had never pretended interest in men, but eighteen years ago, nine months after a 'rather distasteful overnighter' with a Dutch sailor passing through Honduras, she'd given birth. If she had been told the sailor's name, she said, she'd forgotten it the moment she realised what she must do in the cause of science. The nameless Dutchman had gone on his way unaware that he had left something of himself with the tanned woman in the broad-brimmed hat first spotted on the quayside haggling with fishermen. Larissa told Aldous and Mimi how she had found a name for her baby son in the history of the Christian church she carried in her knapsack. She had just got to the 7th century and the first Christian king of Northumbria, whose name was Edwin.

'Well, I had to call the kid something,' she said, 'and I thought there were worse names, so Edwin it was. I resisted the "king" part.'

She and Edwin had lived in a village in south Dorset until, achieving the great age of fourteen, he suddenly announced that he had apprenticed himself to a ship's chandler in Weymouth, who would provide digs for him. Just over two years after Edwin's departure, Larissa herself was made unexpectedly homeless when the government requisitioned the village for 'war use'. It was her brother's invitation that had brought her to Withern Rise, where she had remained. Edwin had visited her there just once. His mother gave the impression that more frequent meetings would be overdoing things.

'His father was a sailor, his mother can't bear to be in one place for more than an afternoon,' she told Aldous and Mimi as she rowed towards the town bridge, 'and between us we produced a clerk, albeit one attached to water. He's oddly squat, too, young Edwin, while I'm quite tall, and the sailor wasn't exactly a dwarf. I sometimes wonder if he wasn't swapped at birth. Still talking about your cousin in case you wonder.'

•

Wednesday: 3

Up in the tree, same bough as before, with nothing to do but wait for 'it' to happen, if it was going to, Naia's eyes strayed. She noticed that the leaves seemed less green than usual. Bit on the yellow side, smaller, and not as abundant as you might expect in June. Odd smell too. Sort of mushroomy. Well, I wouldn't look or smell so hot myself, she thought, if I'd been standing in water for days.

She looked at her watch. Nine minutes past. Maybe he hadn't bothered. Amazing that he'd bothered last time really, after what she'd done. She wondered if it would have worked. A touch, switching their lives back. Tempting to try it again. But no, she'd given her word. Stupid. She could live with breaking a promise if it meant getting her—

The tree shivered. Branches rearranged themselves, leaves shifted and brightened, grew in quantity and volume, and she was holding on tight to avoid slipping off. The bough, she noticed, where she hadn't noticed previously, wasn't as long or sturdy in this reality, or as high.

'I thought it wasn't going to work this time,' Alaric said.

'Me too,' she answered. 'Maybe there's something missing today.'

'A factor?'

He was mocking her. She ignored it.

'The boy. Aldous. He was here the other times.'

'Well, we got here, so we don't need him.'

'I think I'll get down,' Naia said.

'I wouldn't,' he said. 'You might be seen.'

'Don't worry, you don't have to come with me.'

'I just meant that it could be a bit tricky if you're seen. We're seen.'

'You'll have to switch on the charm then, won't you?'

Easing herself into the water, she thought her feet would never touch the ground beneath. When they did, the water almost reached her crotch. Joining her, Alaric just cleared the crotch line, but his discomfort increased when, moving forward, the water seeped through the material of his shorts and spread. He made sure to keep well away from Naia in case she reneged on her word.

They lurked for a time within the shadow of the tree, from where they were able to pick out more differences in both house and garden. As well as the maroon shutters at all the upper windows on this side, there was an extra window between the box room and the nearest corner. In their realities, this window had been bricked in about twenty-five years ago. A large rain barrel stood by the kitchen door where they did not have a barrel. There was no garage. They'd already noticed that there were more trees in this south garden. There didn't seem to be many more elsewhere, but substantially more bushes and shrubs struggled to emerge from the floodwater. There were a couple of wooden sheds, too, and a greenhouse, and the rather ramshackle summerhouse Naia had picked out on their first visit.

'Old photos,' she murmured.

'What?'

'The other family album. The old one. Might be straight out of all this.'

There was an earlier photo album in both their realities. The pictures were black-and-white or sepia, and some were badly faded. They showed forgotten aunts and uncles and great-thisses and great-thats they'd only known as elderly near-strangers, or whose lives they'd missed entirely. Several of the earliest pictures were of a proud young man in army uniform, gangling, bright eyed, a hint of moustache. This was Roderick Lyman Underwood. Their mothers had discovered, during their early researches for the family tree, that Roderick was killed in Flanders in November 1917, at the Battle of Passchendaele. He was eighteen. His early death was a major turning point in

Underwood family history. If Roderick hadn't died when he did, a year before the end of the Great War, Withern Rise would have eventually gone to him instead of to A.E., his younger brother, and an alternative branch of the family would have dwelt there over the years. Because different meetings, liaisons and connections would have occurred in the line which, in this scenario, would not have occupied Withern Rise, Alexandra Bell would not have met Ivan Charles Underwood in 1987 and a year later had a child by him – and neither Alaric or Naia would have been born at all. Unless, of course, there were alternative versions of Roderick and only one of them survived.

The old album contained photographs of the exterior of the house, or bits of it. It never appeared as anything more than a fragmented backdrop for snaps of people in the garden. But Naia was right. What little the album showed of the house was more like this one than either of theirs.

'I don't get it,' Alaric said.

'If it's what I'm thinking, neither do I,' Naia said.

'What are you thinking?'

'I told you, I wanted to check the family tree first.'

'Well, didn't you?'

'My album's disappeared. Your father lost it.'

'Your father now.'

'Don't rub it in.'

'We can't just stand here,' Alaric said. 'Anyone could see us.'

'They might be out,' Naia said.

'All seven of them?'

She shrugged. 'Family trip somewhere?'

'By water?'

'Who knows? We could always knock on the door.'

'I thought they were out.'

'I said they *might* be out.'

'If they are in, they're not going to open the door and let all the water in.'

'A window then, if we see someone inside.'

'So we knock on the window and someone answers. Then what? Introduce ourselves? Tell them we're family from a couple of other dimensions and shake hands all round?'

'We can't say where we're from,' Naia said. 'Wouldn't believe us anyway. No, we just get into some sort of general conversation and see what we can— '

'Can I help you?'

A man leaning out of an upstairs window.

'Time to wing it,' Naia muttered, starting towards the house.

After a pause, Alaric followed, reluctantly.

•

Wednesday: 4

Larissa had rowed them to the town bridge and some way beyond when she turned into the bank and lodged the boat within a semi-circle of bulrushes. 'Remind me of the Nile Delta, these things,' she said, taking a pair of secateurs from a leather satchel. 'Moses, and all that malarkey.' She cut a dozen bulrushes and placed them on the floor of the boat, warning her passengers to mind their feet.

The bank on the Great Parr side of the bridge was a little higher, so the water covered less. Had they wished, they might have climbed onto it and trodden dry land for a change, but they chose to remain in the boat. Just as Aldous and Mimi began to wonder what they would do next, their aunt produced a small muslin bag which, opened out, revealed several dozen bright green gooseberries.

'I salvaged these last week, just before the flooding,' she said, distributing them. 'They've been sunning themselves on my window ledge ever since.' She bit one in half with her front teeth and savoured it. 'Oh, I do love early gooseberries. Not quite as ripe as you might like, perhaps, but...try them.' She swallowed the other half with relish. 'Sour, hard and hairy. Reminds me of Edwin's father, but I'd rather have a gooseberry.'

Aldous and Mimi tried one each. Larissa chuckled

when their cheeks hollowed. After the first taste they nibbled politely rather than pop them whole into their mouths, as they might a month from now.

'Gooseberries are sometimes called fayberries, you know,' their aunt told them, blithely tucking in without a shudder. 'Fayberries, fairyberries, because it was believed – once upon a time – that fairies sheltered in the prickly bushes from predators like us. My granny, Elvira, informed me at a very tender and gullible age that I was born under the gooseberry bushes of Withern Rise. Took me years to realise that there was a problem with that. Probably scarred me for life.'

Tart and juiceless as the gooseberries were, to Aldous and Mimi, in a boat away from home, they were a rare gift. Nibbling and grimacing on the still water, beneath a cool white sun, cream sky, there was an air of calm that felt timeless and complete, until Larissa's urgent whisper:

'Squirrel!'

A small, red, bushy-tailed creature had tripped down a pine tree to nibble a cone gripped in its claws. 'Rodents, I know,' Larissa whispered as Aldous and Mimi leant forward for a better view, 'but I'm rather fond of the little blighters. I lived for a while in Ontario, you know. Log cabin by a lake, heavenly until winter came, then I would head south, to Florida, until the warmth returned. I had a companion called Tallulah at the time, lovely lass, glorious hair, writing a book about British women who settled in Canada in the late eighteen eighties. One spring at the lake, while Lulah was with me, I found a baby squirrel in the grass. He was quite tiny; so new that his eyes were still shut. I picked the little thing up and fed him, kept him in the bedroom, and he thrived. He became very attached to me. I called him Scallywag. Scally for short.

'That Fall,' Larissa went on, quietly so as not to disturb the nibbling squirrel, 'I took Scally outside and put him in a tree and told him to go find his own kind. He wouldn't leave. Absolutely refused. I tried this any number of times, but he simply wouldn't go, preferring to tuck himself inside my shirt or under my arm. I tried taking a branch into the house to get him used to trees, but he wasn't interested unless I was on the branch with him. Lulah found that *highly* amusing! When he could get away with it, Scally slept in my sweater drawer. Sometimes I would take out a jumper and he would tumble onto the floor. Outside the cabin, he would race around my body as if I were a tree and jump on my shoulders – Tallulah's too, when she was working – and rummage in our pockets for peanuts and acorns.

'Fortunately, just before we went south that year,

Scally at last took to the trees. Vanished without so much as a farewell twitch of the tail. Surprising how much that hurt. But the following spring when I returned – minus lovely Lulah – I was talking to an elderly neighbour who lived year round along the lake, and he told me that one morning he was sitting outside eating his breakfast and a red squirrel jumped onto his shoulder and tried to burrow into his pocket. It could only have been my Scallywag.'

As Larissa finished her story, the squirrel on the bank became aware of watching eyes. It tossed the pine cone in the air and shot up the tree as though fired from a gun. Larissa glanced at Aldous and Mimi. They had never seen such a smile on her face. Within a swathe of bulrushes, one pale June day when the water was high, a boy and his young sister sat in a nook of tranquillity that would stay with them for life. Lives which might extend into old age, or end tomorrow.

Wednesday: 5

Naia approached the house, Alaric in her wake. 'We were looking for Aldous,' she said to the man at the window.

'You've missed him. He's off boating with his aunt and sister. Anything I can do?'

'Not really. We were just going to hang out.'

'Hang out?'

'Pass the time.'

Another face appeared in the window, below the first: a small boy who didn't want to miss anything.

'I don't think I know you,' the man said.

'No. Probably not.'

'Bit old for friends of my son's, aren't you?'

Naia glanced at Alaric as he drew alongside, at a calculated arm's reach. He offered no inspiration.

'We were staying with relatives when the floods came,' she told the man, 'and then we couldn't go home. We met Aldous a couple of days ago. He was in his boat.'

'He wasn't allowed beyond the gate,' the man said dubiously.

'We met him *at* the gate. We were just passing. He said we ought to pop in and say hello next time we were…you know.'

It sounded dodgy even to her, but the man evidently decided to accept it, for he said: 'Wait a tick, I'll come down. I was going to collect the eggs anyway.'

'Daddy, Daddy, me too,' the small boy said.

The man laughed. 'Could you catch this? Got to bring my lad, it seems.'

A wicker basket tumbled through the air. Naia

lurched sideways and lost her footing. Missing the basket, she automatically reached out to save herself, caught Alaric's arm before he could step away. He would have shaken her off, but she maintained her grip to pull herself upright.

'You'd see me drown, wouldn't you?' she said.

'I caught you, didn't I?'

'I caught *you*. But at least we know now that touching doesn't do anything here.'

'There is that.'

'Sorry!' Naia called to the window, holding up the dripping basket.

'Never mind, doesn't have to be dry,' the man said, popping a leg over the sill. He stepped cautiously onto the ladder, his little boy astride his neck, and backed slowly down, rung by careful rung.

'What do we do now?' Alaric whispered.

'Act as if we belong here,' Naia replied. 'In this reality.'

The man, in chest-high one-piece black waders, lowered himself into the water. 'This is Ray,' he said, patting his son's knee.

Naia smiled. 'Hello, Ray. How are you?'

'I'm very well, thank you,' the boy said. 'How are you?'

'I'm very well too.'

'How are you?' he asked Alaric.

'Stunning,' Alaric grunted.

'Unusual,' the man said.

Alaric followed his gaze to his ordinary cotton shirt, ordinary wet shorts.

'What is?'

Instead of explaining or making further comment, the man asked if they would like some eggs to take home.

'Oh, I don't think we need any,' Naia replied.

'Course you do. Everyone needs eggs. This way.'

Alaric glanced about him with studied indifference as they followed the man and his son round to the front of the house. Naia, more inquisitive, missed little. They were wading past the front door when the man began singing.

'O, there was an old man named Michael Finnegan,'
He grew whiskers on his chin again...'

The visitors exchanged amused glances. The amusement became dismay when the croaky little voice of the boy joined in.

'The wind came out and blew them in again,
Poor old Michael Finnegan...begin again.
There...was an old man named...'

There were a number of notable differences between their versions of the house and this. The window surrounds were varnished, there were painted lead drainpipes instead of black PVC ones, no front porch. The door between the main entrance and the kitchen intrigued Naia, if not Alaric. At her Withern Rise, and his, there was no door here, only a vertical discolouration where there'd once been one. This door was a –

'He ran a race and thought he'd win again,
Got so puffed that he had to go in again,
Poor old Michael Finnegan…begin again.
There…was an old man named…'

– very unassuming one, which opened precisely where, in both their homes, a large Welsh dresser stood. She remembered her father saying that his parents had extended the kitchen, which could mean that this door opened into a narrow vestibule, where bikes or tools or somesuch were stored, from which the kitchen might be reached by a further door.

They passed the turf-covered metal hut, over the door of which hung a sheet of coarse brown leather. Naia would have asked about the hut if not for the singing, which, from his tormented expression, was getting on Alaric's nerves.

'He got drunk from drinking gin again,
Thus he wasted all his tin again,
Poor old Michael Finnegan…McGinnegan.'

The verse ended as they reached a wooden shack with windows of wire mesh which occupied part of the space where Naia and Alaric were used to seeing a garage. As his father unhooked the gate, the boy on his shoulders turned to look at Naia, immediately behind them. Up close, she noticed that he had a dimple in his left cheek and startlingly blue eyes, a combination which jogged something in her, though she failed to pin it down before the father made some bland comment about the floods, which she felt an obligation to respond to.

There'd been no barrier to keep the water out of the hen house, but there were straw-filled shelves around the walls, where the birds perched and slept and laid their eggs. Naia and Alaric waited outside while the man and his son ducked through the door. The chickens became excited when they entered, but soon settled down. They hadn't been fed any less promptly during the floods. Grain and meal had been spread daily along their beds, instead of scattered haphazardly across the ground, so they were inconvenienced hardly at all.

'They're better off than us,' the man said. 'The house was flooded too, but no one came to feed us. Water get into yours, did it?'

'A bit,' Naia said.

'Only a bit? You're lucky. Lot of folk in the village are forced to live upstairs, like us. The wife hasn't been down since it started.'

All the time his father was collecting the eggs, the boy barely took his eyes off Naia and Alaric. Alaric hated being stared at, even by a kid, and looked away. It was while Naia was returning that curious gaze, forcing a smile, that she realised what it was about the boy. 'My God,' she said, and with the realisation several things clicked into place at once.

The father turned, raised his eyebrows at her. 'Pardon?'

'Nothing. I just remembered that we promised to be home by now.'

'Well, let's get to the kitchen and find something to put some of these in.' Closing the door behind him, he said, 'Bye for now, pretties,' and began wading back to the house. As they followed, Naia looked about her with new eyes, very wide eyes, taking in every visible detail.

'O, there was an old man named Michael Finnegan,'

'Bloody hell,' Alaric muttered as the boy again joined in.

'He went fishing with a pin again,
Caught a fish and dropped it in again,
Poor old Michael Finnegan…McGinnegan.'

The man pushed the kitchen door back and entered. The water was as high inside as out. Again, Naia and Alaric remained outside, he showing his customary lack of interest while she was still too bemused by the flash of intuition at the hen house to realise that she was standing on tiptoe and craning her neck to peer in. It wasn't much like the kitchen she knew. No fitted cupboards and units; instead, open shelves and free-standing cabinets. The sink was a large white enamel job with wooden drainers on either side, and there was an old range, huge and black, instead of a modern gas or electric cooker. No sign of a fridge or freezer.

'Can't we just go?' Alaric whispered.

'What?'

'Let's go,' he hissed.

'Where to?'

'I don't know. Anywhere. The tree?'

'And do what? Wait to be whisked back where we came from?'

'What else?'

'You've no idea, have you?' Naia said.

'What about?'

She nodded at the man in the kitchen sorting through the eggs, his son still on his shoulders, leaning over to count them into a small bag.

'Haven't you noticed anything about the boy?'

'Like what?'

'I mean does he remind you of anyone?' His expression provided the answer. 'When they come out,' she said, 'give him a good look.'

Alaric scowled. 'Why do you always do this? Throw me a hint and ask me to work it out. Always some sort of test with you, isn't it? If you know something, tell me.'

'All right. I think he's Grandpa Rayner.'

'Uh?'

'I think the boy is Grandpa Rayner. Want me to say it again?'

'Grandpa Rayner? But…he was an old man.'

'Not so old.'

'And he died.'

'Yes.'

'But for that kid to be Rayner, this would have to be…'

He might have completed the sentence, and they would certainly have discussed the matter further, but for a shift in the light and a switch of surroundings. Two switches.

'Here we are,' A.E. said, emerging from the kitchen with the bag of eggs. He looked about. So did little Ray. Their visitors had gone.

'Look up!' cried a voice before they could express surprise.

Father and son looked up.

'Step back!' the voice commanded.

They stepped back.

'Wave!'

They waved.

'Smile!'

They smiled.

Marie, leaning out of a first-floor window, took a snapshot with her husband's Baby Brownie. Some months from now she would put the small black-and-white print in the family album with tears in her eyes. Everything would be seen through tears then.

Wednesday: 6

The only thing that hadn't changed was their proximity to the house. The kitchen door, of a slightly different style, was closed, the water level was lower, and they were alone, Naia in her reality, Alaric in his. Their bodies sagged, as if their bones had softened in the transition, and it was a real effort to get to the open window in the Long Room and climb in. Alex was in the utility room, so Alaric wasn't seen, but Naia was.

'Naia, what is it?' Kate said.

'It's all right, I... Wooh!'

Kate helped her out of the waders and guided her to the couch, arm round her shoulders.

'Have you had some sort of accident? Or shock?'

'No, I came over dizzy, that's all. It'll pass.'

'You're sure?'

'It's OK. I just need to sit here for a while. Quietly.'

'Anything I can do?'

She shook her head. Kate left her, reluctantly. Naia lay back and closed her eyes. What caused this? And was it just her, or was Alaric affected the same way after these trips?

Wednesday: 7

Alaric made it up to the bathroom unseen. He took his shorts off with great difficulty and dried his legs. Then, along the landing to his room, wishing he could just crawl there. Inside, he closed the door, very quietly, and lowered himself onto his bed. There he lay panting as though his oxygen supply had been halved without warning. What caused this? And was it just him, or was Naia affected the same way after these trips?

He closed his eyes.

Wednesday: 8

When Naia woke there was a mug of chocolate on the coffee table near her head. She sat up and put the mug to her lips. The chocolate was cool, it had been there for some time, but still good. After a while she felt strong enough to manage the stairs. She reached the landing just as Alaric, in his reality, got off his bed and moved towards the door. He stepped outside. At the very same instant, they both headed for the box room.

On an otherwise clear wall in both box rooms there was a rack of metal shelves, put up by two Alex Underwoods on October 29th 1998 as repositories for jigsaws, board games, and odds and ends that had no place elsewhere. On the top shelf there was a handful of dog-eared pamphlets and books. The books included an enormous (and out-of-date) *Atlas of the Universe*, David Lewis's *On the Plurality of Worlds*, the *Punch* annual of 1890, an edition of *Baedeker's Italy*, published in 1981, and the old family album. On the top shelf of one reality, but not the other, there was also a stamp album. Inside the cover of this, in the artless handwriting of a young boy, was the inscription 'A.U., Withern Rise'.

Unaware of their impeccable timing, Naia and Alaric took down the old photo albums and carried them to their rooms. There, seated in their identical chairs, they began their search for faces, names and clues.

•

Wednesday: 9

Naia often went into the garden when she had some problem to resolve, but walking through high water was hard work, so when she came to the upturned rowing boat on the slope above the landing stage she welcomed it as a place to sit. The repetitive call of a pigeon on the roof, and evening light like old parchment, soothed her. At certain times, and this was undoubtedly one of them, the garden at Withern Rise felt as solitary as any place on earth. Naia had never been afraid of solitude, but tonight she would have valued company. Alaric's company. She needed to talk about the things on her mind. She imagined they were on his mind too, though she couldn't be sure. Alaric still seemed to keep himself to himself, suspicious of fanciful flights of the imagination, inspired conclusions. Even so, likely as he was to be unpleasant and snide rather than amiable and chatty, he was still the only person anywhere who wouldn't think she was stark staring bonkers to talk of such things.

Separately, they'd got enough information out of the old family album to convince them of who they'd met in the other reality. Most of the photos were untitled, undated, but they had come across two with the name 'Rayner' written underneath. One was of a putty-faced baby in a crocheted shawl and someone's arms; the other of a boy of four or five sitting on the garden swing, an older sister standing beside him, frowning for the lens. It was a third picture that clinched it. This one was captioned: *The Floods, June 1945*. Here, the boy sat on his father's shoulders. The man wore high rubber waders, and stood in water that reached his groin, a small paper bag in one hand. They both waved and smiled up at the camera, situated somewhere above them. There was no doubt in Naia's mind, or Alaric's now. The small boy who had found them so fascinating that morning was the grandfather they'd last seen five years ago, aged sixty-two, on his premature deathbed. The man whose shoulders he rode, in whose song he had joined, was their great-grandfather, Alaric Eldon.

Sitting on the boat gazing across a lake which had been a river all her life, thoughts tumbled through Naia's head like loaded dice. Three times, she and Alaric had visited another period of time, not an alternative reality – unless time *was* another form of reality. There was scope here for considerable contemplation, but what interested her more for the moment was one of the people they'd met there. Not her grandfather, but his older brother, Aldous. In the cemetery of her old reality there was a grave whose headstone declared that an Aldous Underwood was buried there. The year of death was given as 1945. She assumed – because it was all she could do without more precise information – that he was eleven when he died. If the Aldous whose bones lay beneath that stone was the one with the boat, he'd had very little time to live when she and Alaric met him. He hadn't looked like someone about to snuff it from some illness or disease, which suggested that something happened in the weeks or months following their meeting. Something fatal.

After a while she got up and walked along the bank, stooping occasionally to trail her hands in the water. She was puzzled by her earlier fatigue. She'd felt dopey enough after the other trips, but this time she'd been totally knocked out. Why? When she'd passed from her reality into Alaric's back in February, there'd been the most appalling pain, but it had stopped as soon as she arrived there. There'd been no pain before these recent visits, hardly any sensation at all, but when she *returned*! So what was the difference? Well, there was one quite obvious difference. There'd been no time differential between her reality and Alaric's. They lived parallel existences, minute for minute; but the recent journeys had been to another day. Another decade. She smiled. Naia Underwood: Time Traveller. It was a short-lived smile. Whatever it was about the trips to 1945 that brought about such dreadful feebleness, she didn't fancy experiencing it again in a hurry. Curious as she was about life at Withern Rise back then, she would *not* be shinning up that tree for a day or two.

The tree. The envelope in the message hole. With so much going on it had slipped her mind. She rounded the corner of the house and entered the south garden. At the Family Tree she removed the envelope. As she was doing so she had the oddest feeling of being watched, and turned just in time to see binoculars lowered amid the bushes and trees along the drive. She glimpsed a face. A man's. A stranger's.

'Excuse me?' she said loudly.

He said nothing; scurried away. She heard him splashing towards the gate. Now what was *he* up to?

She shrugged. In summer, people often darted up the drive for a peep at the house, not because it was particularly striking or grand, but simply because it was there. Such intrusions were taken for granted without being welcomed, but for someone with no business there to broach the drive when it was under water suggested an even greater degree of nosiness than usual. And he had binoculars. Peeping Tom? She would have to warn Kate.

Reaching the house, Naia climbed in the window, a routine mode of entry by now, and removed the waders. A minute later, up in her room, she broke the seal of the envelope. Inside, she found a folded sheet of paper covered in typing. Same primitive manual typewriter as before, but she'd been wrong about the content. It wasn't the same at all.

<u>WARNING</u>

Entire worlds, whole universes, identical in most prominent details, co-exist within a hair's breadth of one another. The realities go about the construction of their histories without any more awareness of each other than a flea is aware of communication satellites.

This is just as well.

Imagine if we all knew that alternative versions of ourselves were washing their hair at the instant we were washing ours, eating a boiled egg when we were eating one, or, for that matter, sitting on the lavatory while we were taking a shower. For the most part the realities do not overlap or encroach, but there are some which draw you into them. These are almost always earlier realities which continue to exist when standard time moves on.

They are dangerous. Resist them if you can.

Aldous U.
Withern Rise

Naia read the document several times. Unlike the first one it seemed to be directed specifically at her. And the reference to non-parallel realities, earlier realities, sounded as if the writer knew she'd been to one. The writer. Obviously the old man who called himself Aldous Underwood. If the name wasn't enough, she'd seen him leaving the tree just before she found the envelope. The one time she'd met him he hadn't seemed particularly bright. How could someone like him even *think* this way, let alone know so much? There must be more to him than met the eye; or more than he let on. And what did he mean by that warning? What harm was there in these...time-realities?

She needed to ask these things face to face; hear what he knew from his own lips – and find out why versions of him in two realities were writing such things and putting them in the Family Tree. She hoped also to learn, in a chat with him, if he was the boy she and Alaric had met in 1945. And if he was, whose grave it was in the cemetery of her old reality.

Wednesday: 10

For much of today Aldous had made a point of wandering where the floodwater was highest. Unlike Naia, it did not occur to him that he might slip or stumble and go under. The new waders gave him the confidence to go wherever he pleased, short of the actual river, and he intended to make the most of them. Before the floods he'd walked for miles every day, with a young man's energy, rediscovering parts and places unrecalled till he saw them again. The town ended where a weekly livestock market once flourished. His father used to take him to the market to watch the bidding for horses, sheep, pigs, poultry, and he fancied he could smell it even now, though a squat block of offices now occupied the site. Then over a cattle grid, and he was truly out of town, on Cow Common, where cattle still grazed, though fewer than when he came here with Father or Maman. The path through the common ran all the way to the old paper mill, in the process of being demolished to make way for an industrial estate. Half a mile on, at a token stretch of the old Great North Road, he would head across country towards Eaton Fane, Great Parr, or one of the other villages which, since his time, had become thoroughfares thick with cars, bordered by bland modern housing.

But, mid evening now, and after all that trudging through water he was feeling the age he looked. He decided to turn in. Getting out of the water and into the hammock was never easy, but it was even more difficult with the new boots. Hauling himself up and removing the boots without getting his bedding wet was quite a task, but, managing it, he lodged the boots in the branches to the right of his head, as he'd done last night, and lay down to wait for sleep. It was still a novelty not to fear sleep, and every now and then he would wake in the night trembling from a dream that had returned him to the clinic and all it represented. Last night he'd woken like this and almost fallen out of the hammock upon seeing, in the dim light, the shape of some monster about to pounce. It was the boots, but his nerves took several minutes to settle.

Tonight he'd just got comfortable when his beloved gran came into his mind. He remembered how she used to tuck him in and sit by his bed, reading stirring tales of giant killers and boys living in the jungle, of Viking marauders, quests for holy grails, adventures on the high seas. He could still hear her voice, the melodic tone of it, the chuckle when she read an amusing passage. He saw himself, lying there, taking it all in, curtains drawn back so that he could gaze at the barely moving reflections cast by the water below the window of his corner room. Gran's voice. Gran's stories. Gran's lips on his forehead.

'Night, Tommy.'

His pleasant drowsiness burst like a pricked balloon.

Tommy? Gran had never called him Tommy. It wasn't his name, so why would she? He was Aldous. Aldous Underwood of Withern Rise, and he was eleven years old. And he was going to die tomorrow.

THURSDAY

Thursday: 1

Larissa had summoned her brother and his wife and the four children to the kitchen to announce her decision. Larissa was fond of the kitchen, with its enormous range and flagstone floor, the walk-in pantry, the Sheila Maid on pulleys. She was often to be found here, deep in the old rocking chair, feet on a stool in woollen half socks (toes arranged in neat, naked rows) while she read an Austen, a Trollope or a Galsworthy. Once a small speckled frog had hopped through the open door while she was thus engaged, whereupon she leapt up and chased it round and round the table, without much idea what she would do if she caught it. Decision was not called for, however, for on its final circuit the impertinent creature hopped out of the door and across the garden.

'You're leaving for France?' A.E. said on hearing the

news. 'Liss, there's been a war in Europe, haven't you heard?'

'The war in *Europe* is over,' she replied firmly. 'So I can travel freely once more.'

'Why France?'

'I had a friend there, in a little village near Poitiers. I want to see if she survived the...hostilities.' The last word was uttered with steely disdain.

'Poitiers?' Marie said with a flash of interest. 'Poitiers is little more than a hundred kilometres from Limoges.'

'What about it?' Larissa said.

'Well...I'm from Limoges.'

'I'm aware of that, dear, but your place of birth has nothing whatever to do with my reason for going somewhere else entirely, whatever the proximity.'

'No, no, of course, I just...'

'Quite,' said Larissa, concluding that part of the discussion.

'You haven't heard from this friend?' A.E. asked her.

'Until France capitulated we wrote all the time. Her letters ceased quite suddenly then.'

'Did you keep writing to her?'

'For a few months. It began to seem pointless when there were no replies.'

'When will you come back?' Mimi asked, eyes very large and shiny.

Her aunt stretched forth a long arm. Mimi stepped forward.

'I can't say, dear. I'll write. Postal services should be back to normal before too long.'

Mimi bit her lip. 'Letters won't be the same.'

Then Larissa did something that startled everyone. She took Mimi's head between her two hands, drew it down to her mouth, and kissed her tenderly on the forehead. Then she folded the girl into her arms and held her close, gently stroking her hair. Such displays of affection from this self-possessed, occasionally formidable woman were unprecedented. Never before had she kissed one of the children in public, even Mimi. No one knew where to look, except A.E., who turned to the window. He was fond of his big sister. She had pampered him when he was little.

'When will you be leaving?'

'In a day or two. I have passage to arrange.'

He cleared his throat. 'We'll miss you.'

'You'll get over it,' said Larissa.

Thursday: 2

Stone Public Library was not a regular haunt of Alaric's, but today he had a mission: to see what he could learn about life in Eynesford in the mid-1940s. He might have obtained more information online, but Ivan's broadband connection was down, and he didn't own a computer himself; never wanted one, had enough of the damn things at school. There were computers in the library, of course, but he hated looking stuff up in public places. Never knew who might suddenly be standing behind you. You didn't have to be scanning porn to be self-conscious about being watched.

To get to the library he had to wade through the village, into Parable Road by St Cecilia's, past a breaker's yard, a small graphic design studio, and a fine Georgian residence which had recently been turned into solicitors' offices. To his left, here, the narrow tributary that had once fed the woodyard was contained by a steep bank of earth and grass. Other parts of the town, like the village, had not been so well protected. At the end, where the road turned sharp right towards the junction with the High Street, he stopped before a large grey slate set into the wall beside the steps of the marina bridge. Etched into the slate were markers showing the flood levels reached in June 1945 and March 1947. The later level beat the earlier by some way, which meant that the waters of 1945, which were higher than his own, would be superseded just two years later.

He continued on to the library.

•

Thursday: 3

Naia had no idea where to look for the old boy. He could be anywhere. All she could do was walk around and hope to come across him. The water was a bit lower today. Plants that had been completely covered were struggling to reveal themselves once more. Making her way round the vegetable garden and out of the side gate, she was about to start up the lane to the village when a voice hailed her.

'Naia! Taking the waters?'

She looked back. Mr Knight had turned the corner, where the river path was until a few days ago. She hesitated. Mr Knight was a nice man, but it wasn't always easy to think of something to say to someone that old. The reason she didn't rush away was that she'd seen him with the man she was looking for. She wasted no time getting to the point when he reached her.

'You mean Aldous?' Mr Knight said when she put her first question.

'Yes. If that's his real name.'

'Why shouldn't it be?'

'Well...you know...Underwood?'

'I don't know him that well myself,' Mr Knight said. 'We walk together sometimes. That's it really. We don't go on pub-crawls or to the dog track.'

'But you talk,' she said. 'While you walk.'

'Oh yes, we're multi-talented.'

'Well he must have told you stuff.'

'Stuff?'

'About himself.'

Mr Knight looked down at her. She was tall, but he was taller, broad-shouldered, with thick grey hair, swept back, a prominently bridged nose, and a mouth that seemed constantly on the verge of smiling but rarely did. It was a generous face, friendly enough, but the face of one used to keeping his own counsel.

'Why don't you just come out and say what you're after, girl?'

'I don't know what I'm after,' she confessed.

'Well, that's that then.'

He continued along the lane. Naia rushed to catch him, fell in watery step with him. 'But his name,' she said. 'If that's his name, and he's from round here, wouldn't he have to be…a relative?'

'Seems likely.'

'Oh, please. Tell me what you can.'

He glanced at her, but did not stop. 'Whatever Aldous might have told me about himself, he didn't give me permission to broadcast it far and wide.'

'I won't tell a soul,' Naia said.

'Maybe not, but if you want to know anything about him, you must get it from him.'

'But I don't know him. I've only spoken to him once.'

'He's quite harmless,' Mr Knight assured her.

'I did wonder.'

'Not used to people, that's all. Shy. Had a sad life.'

Her interest quickened. 'Sad? Tell me.'

He shook his head. 'Not my place. Wouldn't feel right about it.' They had reached the end of the lane and he was about to leave her, but paused. 'You know about his living conditions?' She shook her head. 'He lives out of doors. Just across the river from you.'

'He *what*?'

Mr Knight told her about the hammock, and where it was hung. She was astonished.

'Is he so poor that he can't afford a room or anything?'

'I don't think he lives in the open out of poverty,' Mr Knight said.

'What then?'

'Doesn't like to feel enclosed. And he's not so badly off now the trees are full. He's fairly sheltered there.'

'But all the water,' Naia said.

'Doesn't seem to worry him.'

He turned away, and with a high wave set off along the village street.

•

Thursday: 4

Stone Library, red-brick, imposing, and raised above the water level by a series of steps, dated back to mid-Victorian times. It was not a vast library but it was reasonably well-stocked, and the staff were amiable. Alaric was directed to a section in which he found a number of information books about the area. Among these were a handful of thin volumes by 'local authors' which dealt with the histories of Stone, Eynesford, Eaton Fane and neighbouring villages. In one an entire chapter was devoted to the floods of '45 and '47. One of the reasons given for the river's tendency to rise so significantly and rapidly during those years was the town bridge. Built in a less frantic period, when fewer demands were made upon it, the bridge was at that time supported by a series of narrow arches which prevented the river from flowing as freely as it needed to following heavy rains. In the early 1950s the bridge was rebuilt, with fewer supports, and flooding ceased to be a threat – until now.

Summer flooding had never been a common occurrence, but until modern times the Great Ouse burst its banks during many a winter. The winter of 1947 saw flooding of epic proportions. Thick ice and snow from January onwards had brought much of the area to a standstill. But then, in the middle of March, a very fast thaw set in. Snow and ice melted quickly, the river rose dramatically, and within two days the area was badly flooded. The waters of this and the flood of two years earlier found their way into more than half the buildings of Eynesford and Stone. Shops and business premises were summarily closed and householders driven into the upper reaches of their homes. The water was so deep that at one location (a cottage in a dell near the church at Eaton Fane) an elderly lady by the name of Mrs Grieves heard a tapping sound at her bedroom window, and, turning, found a swan pecking at the glass. Horse-drawn farm carts with huge wheels were brought in to ferry people around parts of the town, and between villages. Where the water was slightly shallower, lorries were used as buses. Many people got about by boat. Shopkeepers went house-to-house in punts, dinghies and rowing boats, ringing bells to draw people to upper windows. Provisions were hauled or handed up on poles, brooms or other useful implements. One enterprising baker raised his wares on a hod borrowed from his bricklayer son-in-law.

Small black-and-white photos were dotted throughout the chapter on the flooding. Stone market place was clearly recognisable in the largest of them. Alaric also recognised several of the shop fronts, in spite of the changes made to them since the nineteen forties. Interesting as many of the pictures were, there was one that caught his attention above all the others. This showed the lane in Eynesford that ran past the primary school down to the river. The lane, like the playground, was under water, and a young woman was walking along it, towards the camera. She held one arm across her middle, holding something inside her coat by the look of it, while the other was half raised, slightly blurred, as if waving the photographer away. The shape of her mouth suggested that she was speaking or shouting at the instant the shutter clicked. But what caught Alaric's eye was that the girl was a dead-ringer for Naia. Of the many faces he'd studied in the old photo album none were this much like hers. There was no name under the photo in the library book, but she had to be an Underwood, looking like that. The question was, which Underwood? And why were there no pictures of her in the old album?

Thursday: 5

Naia spent much of the morning and some of the afternoon looking for the old man who, she had no doubt now, really was called Aldous Underwood. The one place she deliberately avoided was his 'home' across from the house. Even if he was there, it would be too much of an intrusion to walk in on him. It wasn't like knocking on a door after all.

Thursday: 6

Larissa was jubilant. A rare mood in everyone's experience but her brother's. Only he had known her as an excitable girl and impulsive young woman. To him, the reason for her sudden lifting of spirits was obvious. She was going away. Larissa had grown up at Withern Rise, but it was years since she'd last wanted to stay there for any length of time. 'It *reeks* of childhood,' she once said. Quizzed about her need to be ever on the move, she would claim to be 'stultified' by the idea of passing night after night in the same bed. What made her pulse race was the thought of not knowing where she would be resting on a given or ungiven night.

When A.E. had said that he would miss his sister, he meant it. His wife did not share the sentiment, though she did her best not to let it show. So relieved was Marie that her sister-in-law was going at last that she readily sanctioned Larissa's proposed outing, with all four children, to the Coneygeare and beyond by boat. Even Ursula was keen to join this expedition. Like her mother, Ursula did not feel much affection for her aunt (who'd never shown much for her) but she was leaving now, and it seemed churlish not to go out with her this once.

A.E. carried his children one by one to the boat. He did not carry his sister. Larissa, bootless and stockingless, had tucked her skirts into her knickers to cross the short distance from the porch. 'No room for me, I see,' A.E. said when all five were aboard.

'This is an outing for the fancy free,' his sister informed him.

'Fancy free? What does that make me then?'

'You are a householder, dear boy. You are a husband, a father, an employer. The weight of the world is on your shoulders.'

'I try not to let it show,' he said plaintively.

'Try as you like, it's a fact. Give us a shove.'

He untied the boat, provided the stipulated shove, and stood by the closed French windows of the River Room, watching their departure. This time Larissa allowed Aldous to row.

At one point while they were out, Ray asked to take a turn at rowing. Aldous objected, but when Ray looked like going into a sulk Ursula ordered him to surrender the oars. Aldous knew better than to cross his sister, even though she was a year younger than he, and handed them over. For the next few minutes Ray struggled to control the boat. Aldous had no patience with him.

'We're going in *circles*!' he shouted.

'It's not *my* fault!' Ray shouted back.

'You've got the *oars*!'

'He hasn't done this before,' Ursula said. 'You might tell him how instead of bawling at him.'

'Stop arguing, all of you,' said Mimi.

'Yes, stop arguing,' said Larissa calmly, and she and Mimi nodded at one another as if sealing a covenant.

Ray handed the oars back. Aldous grabbed them eagerly. To show off his comparative skills he rowed around the Coneygeare smoothly and efficiently. There were fewer boats out than the last time he'd done this, with his father. The novelty of boating on water that was commonly open ground was on the wane. Even for those whose premises had withstood the incursion, the flood was now more of a nuisance than a source of amusement. A few still enjoyed it, however.

'Look, there's Mr Knight,' Ursula pointed out.

About eighty yards off, their gardener was rowing his wife and small son this way and that. A family outing on the waters.

'I've never seen Mr Knight's little boy,' Mimi said. 'Can we go and say good afternoon?'

'Mrs Knight won't be keen.'

'I don't care, I want to see the little boy.'

Aldous protested, but was overruled by the girls. Their aunt, herself no drooler over small offspring, withheld her objections.

Mrs Knight was a fairly precise opposite to her husband. Where he was tall, she was short; where he was lean, she was plump; where he was cheerful, she was resolutely doleful of countenance and manner. While Mr Knight greeted the boatload of Underwoods his wife gave the impression that she was rather put out by their approach.

The Knights' cottage was just across from Withern's side gate, but in the three and a half years since their marriage, when she moved to Eynesford from Great Parr, Mrs Knight had not gone out of her way to become friendly with her husband's employers – or their children. The reason for this was a slightly unsavoury family link discovered shortly before her baby's birth. A link which she had no intention of admitting, to the Underwoods least of all, and which she had forbidden her husband to speak of to a living soul.

The two boats jostled one another, bobbed side-by-side as Mimi reached across and touched the boy's chunky cheek. He didn't seem to mind. In fact, he beamed at her. The doting mother softened. The quickest way to Clarice

Knight's heart was to adore her son.

'What's his name?' Mimi enquired.

'He has two,' Mr Knight said with a sly glance at his wife.

She glared back at him. 'We call him *John*.'

'No sense of heritage,' Mr Knight muttered mischievously. While Clarice returned her attentions to their child, who was involved in some sort of dialogue with Mimi, he addressed Larissa. 'I hear you're leaving us, Miss Underwood.'

'News spreads quickly round here,' Larissa said.

'I didn't catch where you're going.'

'France. Initially.'

'France? Wouldn't catch me going there. Lot of clearing up to be done there. Lot of bad feeling.'

'I'll take my chances.'

'Be there long, will you?'

'I can't say. Depends who I find there.'

The gardener nodded as if he understood, though he was only being polite. Ursula and Ray were also chatting to the little boy by this time. Only Aldous remained aloof, staring across the watery plain of the Coneygeare hoping the others would notice before *much* longer that he was keen to be on his way. When all conversation and child-gazing were done, he turned the boat towards the village.

It was four-twenty-five. He had fifty-five minutes to live.

Thursday: 7

After his return from the library, Alaric had gone out of his way to distract himself from what he felt he must do. It wasn't until around five that he at last screwed up the nerve. All right, he said to himself, so I'll be shagged out afterwards, but how often do you get a chance to step into your family's past, for God's sake?

Not that that was why he wanted to get to the 1945 reality. He wanted to see Naia, and that was the only place he was likely to bump into her. He had his family album with him, still in the polythene, unwrapped since its retrieval from the boat-house. He planned to show it to her, if she was there, hoping the sad empty leaves at the end would tug at her heart strings, persuade her to part with the picture-filled pages removed from her album. If she gave him those pages he would be able to add them to his and produce it at last for Alex's inspection. He'd have to lose any shots Naia was in, and somehow explain the gaps, but one thing at a time.

All this depended on their ability to reach the earlier reality at the same point. He might not be able to get there without her, or she without him. She could have been right when she suggested that more than one person might be required to effect the transition. He just hoped she was thinking along the same lines at this moment. He loosened the cord around the covered album, looped it over his shoulder in order to have his hands free, and started to climb.

Thursday: 8

Aldous rowed along the village street, so much wider with the pavements under water. A swan sailed along the middle of this new river, beak turning grandly this way and that on its proud white neck. There were a couple of other boats, whose occupants hailed the Underwood party, as did a group of dedicated strollers in waders. 'Look, a fish!' Ray, said, pointing over the side. People waved from upper windows, not because they were friends but because they too were in thrall to the floods.

Such disasters, being rare, had a way of engendering a camaraderie which kept its head well below the sill at 'normal' times. Three winters ago there'd been extensive power cuts in the area. In Eynesford, people with stocks of candles had handed them round without expectation of reimbursement. One evening, at a couple of hours' notice, there'd been a gathering such as there hadn't been for years, when dozens of candle-toters and bearers of hurricane lamps had congregated in the street, and beer and mulled wine had been provided gratis by the publican of The Sorry Fiddler. There'd been singing and dancing.

Everything was interesting from the boat, especially for the younger children. For them all sorts of things ordinarily taken for granted, or not particularly interesting, suddenly had striking new qualities. But it was the display in the newsagent's window that caught Larissa's eye: an elaborate promotion for the entertainment that should have been with them this week. By now Willy Bright's Circus should have transformed the Coneygeare. A circus would have been a welcome diversion after the austerity and privations of the past few years. A street party had been planned to accompany it. Almost every household had volunteered chairs and tables, to be placed end-to-end along Main Street. But then the Great Ouse got all uppity and that was that. Even though the circus and the party had been cancelled the newsagent's window display remained, and the shop was open. The owner, Mr Bettany, had insisted on keeping normal business hours since the water burst in some days ago, standing behind the counter in his fishing attire (minus the hat) waiting for custom.

Larissa and the three younger children admired the colourful display, part of which declared that a free mask would be offered with every ticket for the circus bought from the shop.

'Masks!' breathed Mimi.

Her aunt leant in the door and asked if the masks were for sale. Mr Bettany told her that if she bought enough sweets he would give them a mask apiece.

'How many must I buy?' Larissa enquired.

'How many coupons have you got?'

'My full quota. And my brother's. I also have actual money...'

A deal was struck, and Mr Bettany scooped the selected sweets out of his enormous glass jars and screwed them into four separate twists of paper. The four clown masks he provided were all different, highly coloured, absurdly manic. 'What about me?' Larissa said. 'Or do I have to buy sweets for myself too?'

Mr Bettany smiled and told her to take her pick. Larissa pointed through the glass at a particularly grotesque object, and the shopkeeper fetched it for her. She put it on at once. Ursula, Mimi and Ray already had theirs on, squeezing sweets through the insane cardboard mouths. Aldous had not yet touched his bull's-eyes, even though they were his favourites after aniseed balls. He also refused to put his mask on. 'I won't be able to see to row,' he said, embarrassed to wear such a thing in public. A friend might catch a glimpse of him. That the friend would probably not recognise him in a clown mask made no difference whatsoever.

From the newsagent's, Aldous rowed the boat round the corner, into the lane that would take them to Withern's side gate.

'It won't go through the gate,' Ursula's muffled voice reminded him.

'I know that. I'll go down to the river and up to the garden from there.'

While Larissa and the younger children played the fool in their masks, occasionally rocking the boat dangerously, Aldous rowed past the allotments and the cemetery and Withern's northern wall. From there he passed over the sunken river bank and onto the wide water, where he swung around and rowed parallel with the garden and the landing stage until he reached the great willow that cornered the south garden.

Twenty minutes to go.

Thursday: 9
Alaric's hope for some sort of psychic synchronicity between himself and Naia was not to be realised. At five past five, as he was climbing the tree, she was

lying on the chaise in the River Room, theoretically reading a book, in practice harassed by salvos of questions. One of the most insistent questions was why the pair of them were able, all of a sudden, to drop into the past without trying. Whatever the reason, and there had to be one, suppose the same thing had happened to others. How many might have found themselves unexpectedly in a time-reality that was not their own? Some might not have lived in the modern era. Might have lived in any age. There they are, minding their own business in the fourteenth century, and a minute later they're being pointed at in the sixteenth or eighteenth. On their return, frightened and baffled, they tell their tale to everyone they meet, to their cost. More often than not, the tellers of such tales would be written off as lunatics, but in some centuries, some cultures, they would be flung into dungeons or executed as subversives by the current oligarchy or regime. Just as well she lived now, and here. Not that she intended to blurt *her* story to the nearest pair of ears.

An even more pertinent question than why she and Alaric were suddenly capable of crossing into another time period was why it was always the same one. Why, three days in a row, on climbing their respective Family Trees, had they been transferred to a single version of the same tree sixty years earlier? The tree. What was it?

Some sort of conduit to other days of its existence? If so, why was it active now, when it had shown no such ability on the numerous occasions she – and Alaric, no doubt – had climbed it when younger? The Family Tree a point of embarkation to other days? Whatever next? Wait, though. Suppose it wasn't that. Not an unofficial customs post between present and past, but an obstruction that wasn't working too well just now. The tree wasn't looking so great at the moment. The floodwater could have weakened it; reduced its effectiveness as a barrier…

Being of a skittish turn of mind, Naia's thoughts leapt unbidden to last August, when she and her parents were holidaying on the island of Rhodes. They'd been staying in Lindos, a sunken little oven of a town dedicated at that time of year to the tourists who flocked in from all over the world. One morning, desperate for a breeze, they drove to Prasonissi, the island's southernmost point, beyond which a sandbank, a thousand metres long, divided the Mediterranean from the Aegean, rolling towards one another in long shallow crested waves. The Aegean was a bit choppy some way out, to the delight of windsurfers, while the Med was fairly unruffled. Glad of the cooler air which made the intense blue heat so much more bearable, Naia left her parents at their rented car and set off along the sandbank, enjoying the fine warm sand between her bare toes. Some way along, the sand narrowed into an elongated spear shape before disappearing altogether, allowing the two great oceans to meet and mingle. She stopped just before the vanishing point, feet straddling the sandbank, comparing the temperatures of the waters. The Mediterranean, she decided, was about two degrees colder than the Aegean.

As an analogy it lacked finesse, but ten months on, in the River Room of a Withern Rise she'd never imagined at that time, she wondered if the barrier that kept the realities apart was all that different from the sandbank between the two oceans. Might there not be a point at which the barrier became so ineffectual that two realities fused? Could it happen? Two similar realities, running side-by-side, like hers and Alaric's, merge without warning, to occupy a single space. Suddenly there's two of almost everything. Everyone. An unexpected doubling of the world's population would make for a pretty crowded planet, and there would be lookalikes all over the place, all trying to occupy the same housing, same jobs, take the same holidays. Poor countries, in which multitudes were already malnourished or starving, would stand half the chance they had before. Mass murderers would have a field day. Religious fundamentalists would say it was God's Work and plant even more bombs.

And what about wars? If the same war was going on in both realities at the time of fusion, would the amount of destruction double, along with the casualties? And the duplication of governments, ambassadors, assorted dignitaries. What about that? Twin Presidents in the Oval Office, two screwed-up British Royal Families, murderous despots trying to rub out their doubles in military dictatorships all over the world. It didn't bear thinking about.

But it didn't stop there. That was just *parallel* realities. What if realities of different *time periods* merged? 1945 and 2005 would be tricky enough, but suppose realities hundreds of years apart found themselves sharing a...

No. Stop. Enough. She needed a break from her own thoughts. She put her book aside and got up. Went to the kitchen and put the kettle on. Mug of fruit tea required. *Cranberry, Raspberry and Elderflower*. Perfect calmer of the wired mind. She hoped.

Thursday: 10

At first when Alaric climbed the tree nothing happened. He imagined this was because Naia wasn't also in her tree. But after sitting there for some minutes he felt the tiny lurch which, a second later, proved that he didn't need her participation at all. He was in the 1945 tree, alone, thinking that he might as well have left the photo album behind. She might yet turn up, though, might even now be climbing hers and in a minute be with him. He waited. The minute passed. And several more. By the end of five he was fed up. What to do? Stay there doing nothing, or get down and slush around the garden? If he did that, he might be seen by someone who didn't know him. He didn't like that idea. Unlike Naia he didn't have a ready answer for everything.

So he decided to stay where he was. Safer. He had no idea how long he would have to remain there, or if he had to do anything to get back. All he could do was wait till it happened. To pass the time he loosened the cord at the neck of the polythene bag and took the album out. He'd intended to look at it anyway sooner or later. He cast about for somewhere to put the bag temporarily. On the bough, some little way along, there was a stump, where a branch had broken off at some stage. He looped the cord over the stump, sat back against the trunk, and began to flip slowly through the visual record of his life.

•

Thursday: 11

Aldous was sick of all the laughter and high spirits, the way they kept wobbling the boat. Rowing was a serious business. Passing into the south garden, he planned to weave in and out of the trees for a while before turning back to the house. If they wanted to stay out after that, one of them could row. But when he saw his own tree, regal and expansive in the water, he felt an urge to be in it. While the kids larked about, and his aunt did nothing to calm them, he rowed towards Aldous's Oak.

Thursday: 12

Alaric looked up from the photographs. Voices. Young, excited voices, but there was a woman's in there too. He closed the album. Tucking it under his arm he climbed higher, into more abundant cover. There he sat, listening, hardly daring to breathe. The voices were directly below him now.

Thursday: 13

Beneath the tree, Aldous offered the oars. 'Here, who wants them?'

'Had enough?' Larissa said.

'Yes.'

She accepted them. Aldous stood up.

'What are you doing?' Mimi demanded through her clown mask.

'Climbing.'

'Ooh, can I climb too?' asked Ray, excited.

'No.'

Gripping the lowest bough, a full stretch above the water, Aldous shoved the boat away with his heels and pulled himself upward.

Thursday: 14

When the tree jolted Alaric thought, with some relief, that he was on his way out of this reality. But nothing changed. It was someone climbing onto the bough below the bank of leaves.

Thursday: 15

Squatting on the bough, Aldoous heard the happy voices of his sisters and brother as they boated around the garden. Larissa rowed in a series of vaguely concentric circles, to the children's delight. Away from them he began to feel rather mean. The others had made an effort today because their aunt was going away. Even Ursula had entered into the spirit of things.

And Larissa. In the village, she had insisted on getting those masks for them. She'd deliberately acted out of character in the cause of making the excursion entertaining and memorable for her nephews and nieces. And he? He had scowled and pouted and refused to participate, or do anything but row the boat. Angry with himself, he raised a foot and kicked the tree as if to blame it for his own selfishness.

As he kicked, Aldous noticed something just to his left. He might have looked either way, but he looked to the left, and this was his undoing. If he had looked to his right he would have been so startled that he would have fallen out of the tree into the water. He would have got up, spluttering, and returned to the house with some haste to dry out. What he would have seen in that glance to the right was a hand, lying palm down alongside his own. The hand was attached to the arm of a boy, sitting on a very similar bough, completely unaware that his hand, *only* his hand, had quirked, briefly, from his reality into another. There was one other thing about the unattached hand that would have startled Aldous if he'd noticed it.

It was green.

The green hand vanished while he focussed on the something he *had* noticed: the polythene bag dangling from the stump a yard to his left.

Thursday: 16

Amid the laughter and frivolity, Ursula glanced back at the tree her brother had climbed into. The leaves concealed him, but he was in there somewhere, and she wanted to let him know that she wasn't pleased with him.

'Aldous is a misery!' she shouted.

Thursday: 17

Alaric heard the taunt; put it down to childish games. He remained absolutely still, back against the trunk, knees drawn up to his chin. A blackbird, strutting through the leaves, evidently did not perceive him to be a threat, and remained, some way along, looking about sharply as if to say, 'Nice here, isn't it?' There was some slight movement below, but as the source could not be seen through the foliage, the bird was not intimidated by this either. It occurred to Alaric that it might be Aldous down there, but he couldn't pull back the leaves to see, in case it wasn't. Nor, for the same reason, could he call out. So he remained where he was.

Quite still.

Until he got cramp.

•

Thursday: 18

'Aldous is a misery!'

Hearing this, Aldous was even more ashamed. If Ursula thought that of him, then the others probably did too. Even his aunt. He didn't feel comfortable as the focus of such opinion. He wanted to repair it; show them that he wasn't really like that.

And he had an idea how to do it.

He unhooked the bag and examined it. He'd never seen material like this. Thick, strong, transparent. But perfect. He seized a fistful of leaves, stuffed them inside, then opened the bag wider and tipped his head into it. He tightened the drawstring just enough to stop the leaves falling out at the neck, threw the loop of the cord over one shoulder like a scarf, and looked about him. Everything was a bit hazy through the strange material, and when he breathed in it followed the breath and clung to his lips. He wished he had a mirror. Oh, how they'd laugh when they saw him in this strange bag with the leaves in his hair!

He peered down at the water. It was a fair drop, but it would be funnier if he made a big splash and rose from the water like some fabulous creature of the deep, pulling a face inside the bag, making monstrous sounds, waving his arms as he loped towards them in the boat. The girls would screech and yell. Aunt Larissa, too, with any luck. He hoped Ray wouldn't have nightmares afterwards. Maman would never let him hear the last of it if he gave Ray nightmares.

Thursday: 19

Every so often the blackbird glanced at the motionless Alaric. Only sharp movements were a threat, but it was as well to keep alert. Alaric was less content. The cramp was worsening. He stretched his leg out, cautiously.

Thursday: 20

Oak leaves and polythene clinging to his cheeks and hair, breathing with difficulty but eager to launch his joke, Aldous prepared to jump.

Thursday: 21

When Alaric shook his foot, the alarmed blackbird lifted its wings and careered away through the leaves. Down below, startled by the spirited rustling, Aldous looked up— and lost his balance. With the misting bag over his head, leaves slipping within it, he couldn't see to grab hold of anything. His proposed downward glide became an oblique plunge, which would have caused him to flop awkwardly into the water if the loop of the cord hadn't caught on the very stump he'd plucked it from a few minutes earlier. The cord slid down the stump, and held. His body weight pulled it taut. The mouth of the bag tightened sharply. Then he was swinging below the bough by the neck, feet inches from the water, unable to make more than the smallest sound.

Thursday: 22

The jolt of the tree and the muted sounds from below were so unexpected that Alaric ceased to notice the cramp. He bent down, pulled a section of greenery aside. At first he saw nothing, but then: a frantic arm. Holding on so as not to fall, he leant further out and saw Aldous thrashing about, a hood of sorts over his head, translucent like…polythene.

Shaken, wasting time in his uncertainty what to do for the best, Alaric lodged the photo album in a nest of branches and dropped onto the lower bough. He moved cautiously along it, until he was within reach of the stump, then, leaning out, reached for the boy's collar, intending to lift him enough to loosen the drawstring and tear the polythene from his—

The light changed with the efficiency of a slap, the

water level dropped, and the hanging boy, a minute from death, vanished.

Thursday: 23

It was Mr Knight who found him. He had come to inspect what he could of the garden that was beneath his reach until the flooding subsided. Marie fainted clean away when she saw the body. Ursula and Mimi were inconsolable. Little Ray could only stare blankly about him, trying to make sense of it all. His brother? Dead? No more Aldous? Impossible!

Larissa blamed herself, and no one had ever seen her so distraught. 'I should never have left him, I should never have left him. Why did I leave him, why did I leave him *alone*? I should be killed! I don't deserve to live!' In other circumstances, her brother would have comforted her. Not today. Alaric Eldon Underwood was already what he would remain until his own early death the following year: a broken man.

Afterwards, Mr Knight told his wife and everyone he met when they asked for details, that 'I damn near died myself when I saw that lad'. The finding of the body would be talked about for many years in Eynesford and Stone, and, to a lesser extent, Great Parr, Eaton Fane and other villages in the vicinity. It wasn't the death so much as the method of it: the peculiar material round his head, the cord drawn taut at the throat, so strong that it had held even against the boy's dead weight.

Thursday: 24

The Westminster clock on the mantelpiece struck seven. Naia glanced at the pale gold face, the stark Roman numerals, the serious arrow-hands, so commanding in that position. Do it, the clock seemed to say. Now is the time. And her mind was made up, yesterday's vow vanquished.

She'd been thinking about little Ray on and off all afternoon. Aldous too, and Withern as it was back then; but Ray most of all. Now that she knew for certain who he was, she wanted to see him again, and soon, even if it meant another incapacitating energy drain afterwards. She might introduce herself this time. She wouldn't be able to say who she actually was, or when she came from, but there was no harm in telling him her name. Her first name anyway. She grinned to herself. If she told him her name he might remember it, and maybe, when he became a grandfather years later, he might suggest Naia as a name for Mum and Dad's newborn baby girl.

She put on the waders that the boy would buy later

in life, climbed out of the window, set off across the south garden. Once in position in the tree, she sat waiting for 'it' to happen, without being totally confident that it would. It did, though, and quickly enough. A tiny lurch, an adjustment of light, and she was in the oak of days gone by. She heard voices. She couldn't make out what they were saying, but they were too close for comfort, so she climbed through the leaves to the next level, where she couldn't be seen if they came nearer. It was there that she saw something very surprising lodged in a network of branches. She stared. No wonder she hadn't been able to find the family album if all the time it had been here. But how could it be here? It wasn't *possible* for it to be here.

But she was too happy to have found it to worry about impossibilities. Time for mysteries later. The voices were drifting away. Tucking the album under her arm, she returned to the lower bough, where she tried to decide what to do. She didn't want to be caught hanging round the garden again. Perhaps she would seem less of an intruder if she was seen emerging from the drive. Depending on who she met, and the story she came up with, she might just be able to engineer a little chat with Rayner, if he wasn't in bed already.

The voices faded. She waited another minute before slipping into the water, where she lingered, peering around to make sure there was no one about before starting towards the bushes that lined the drive. She'd taken just four steps when she heard new voices, from the house this time. Distressed voices. She stopped. Listened hard. Sobbing, wailing, by more than one. Had something happened? Some family argument perhaps. Well, whatever it was, they wouldn't welcome visitors in that mood. She turned around; climbed back into the tree. Ah well. The mission hadn't been a complete failure. She hadn't met young Rayner again, but she'd got the photo album back.

Thursday: 25

Emerging from an exhausted sleep, Alaric was struck by the quality and depth of the silence. Alex and Ivan had been out boating with friends since mid-afternoon, but this wasn't merely the silence of absence or solitude. It was the silence of shock. Or sorrow. Imagination, of course, but that was how it felt to him. On the landing it felt even more intense. The house was riddled with it. As he sank to the floor, still weak, leant against the wall, the boy's face returned to him, as he'd seen it earlier, desperation in the eyes that lifted to him. He saw again the polythene clinging to Aldous's cheeks, covering the open mouth. He could almost feel the throttling cord. A few seconds more and he might have saved him. But there hadn't been any more seconds.

Keen to free himself of this image, this scene, he encouraged his mind to drift. Drifting, a new thought came. A thought so outrageous, but so true, that it shook him to the core: that he personally had provided the instrument of death for his grandfather's older brother, forty-three years before his own birth.

Part Three
LEGACY OF A POET

FRIDAY

Friday: 1

It was only towards the end of the dream that he came to understand that it wasn't a dream at all, but a returning memory. He was wearing something over his head, which clung to his face, limited his vision. He was unable to breathe. His throat was being squeezed as the weight of his body pulled him down. The horror of swinging by the neck from a tree brought him to wide-eyed wakefulness in the sallow light of a new day. Finding himself suspended in a mid-air thick with leaves, he yelped with alarm, tipped sideways, plunged into water. The water did not cover him, but his heart thudded as he sat up, tormented by the images and sensations that had woken him. These faded, however, as physical discomfort achieved dominance. He looked about him. Sniffed. The shallows stank. The water was slimy and dark, dotted with tin cans and other rubbish, the corpse of a large brown rat which he sent on its way with a broken branch.

He got to his feet, stepped out of his enclosure, stooped to wash imagined filth from his hands and clothing. Straightening up, he glanced at the opposite bank. The water level had dropped a little overnight, but the landing stage and the steps and the slope to the house were still covered. His eyes drifted to his old room up in the corner. Someone in the window. He stepped back. The leaves folded about him.

Friday: 2

Naia had woken early for no reason other than that it was light. It was a delicious waking; a leisurely coming to in the sliver of time between night and morning when the world holds its breath and the wrens and blackbirds and thrushes, and all those other hungry attention-seekers, announce their presence, the news and the day. Then the squawks and croaks of the moorhens started, and she opened her eyes and, because she slept with the curtains drawn back, watched the light creep along the walls, the water's reflection dancing across the ceiling. For a little while, lying there, it was as if the past four months had been nothing more than a fiction of a single night. Her mother was asleep along the hall and a good day was about to begin.

But then it was with her again, the actuality, and a swell of sorrow that she quashed at once, to keep it in its place. *This is it. My world. It could be worse. I can handle it. At least I have the house. At least there's Withern Rise.* She focussed on these positives, imposed a necessary perspective on her life as it was now, and kicked the duvet back. She knelt on the bed to look out. The window was open, the way she liked it at night except in the real depths of winter. The air it admitted this morning was as soft and smooth as fine silk. She noticed that the water level was down a bit. The normal world was coming back. Fascinated as she'd been by the changes the floods had introduced, she wasn't sorry. She liked her normal world. Even this one.

She was still at the window when Aldous emerged from cover and scooped water over himself on the opposite bank. She had no explanation for that, seeing as he was fully clothed, and didn't seek one. She'd seen him there, that was what mattered. Odd that she hadn't noticed him before, or, for that matter, any suspicious movement over there. Suddenly she felt quite sorry for him. Living in trees at his age, like a monkey. It wasn't right.

He glanced up. Seeing her watching him, he stepped smartly back. The leaves closed about him like a curtain. Naia remained at the window, and in a few minutes glimpsed him weaving through the thicket. She saw him break out and set off along the bank. The willow between her corner and the water prevented her from seeing further. He might go any of several ways from there, in three different directions across the Meadows, or to the bridge, which would bring him over to her side. Suddenly, now that she knew he was 'out', she was curious to see the old man's domain. She jumped into jeans and a sweater and crept downstairs. In the hall she pulled on Grandpa Rayner's trusty waders, quietly raised the usual window in the Long Room, and clambered over the sill.

Friday: 3

Crossing the bridge, descending once more into water, Aldous followed the line of the path that ran alongside the river towards Withern Rise. Just before the southern boundary wall the path looped to the right, to pass the open five-bar gate. He waded by, with his customary glance along the drive, and within a few paces was turning left towards the old cemetery. In the cemetery he found all the graves visible once more. The ground squelched underfoot, but was no longer covered. An early mist clung to trees and memorials, stealing across the swampy grass. He made his way to the old brick wall that separated the formerly consecrated ground from the house.

The only clear view of Withern at this time of year was from across the river, but that was a bland aspect with the shutters gone and the ivy so orderly. Besides, he saw it all the time. There was more satisfaction in peeking across the vegetable garden from the side gate, struggled-for glimpses over walls, through matted branches, breaks in foliage. Stretching up or round or forward to peer in, he was a boy again, about to run along the path and fling the door back, to be received by his gran with chuckly hugs. But his family no longer lived there. If he were to approach the house and knock, what would he say to the strangers who opened the door? Even if they were Underwoods, as Mr Knight said they were, they weren't his little brother and his sisters, his mother and father, his aunt. Aunt Larissa: what had happened to her? What had happened to any of them? Were any still alive? And if they were, why had they left him at the clinic, turned away from him, as if he were dead?

But this morning he was not seeking glimpses of the house, wallowing in fragments of nostalgia, hoping to claw back more memories. His dream had concerned the tree that bore his name. He'd seen it often enough since his return, at a distance, and more recently close up, by sneaking through the bushes along the drive. But now that he had some idea of the role it had played that last day he needed to see it again.

Reach and crane as he might, he could see very little of the oak from the cemetery, however. Too much else in the way. An apple tree partially overhung the wall. The apples were small, not yet ripe, flecked with dew. He twisted one off at the stem and polished it on his sleeve, reflecting that when he lived at Withern there was a wooden shed here, hard against the wall. Then, quite suddenly, he recalled the gardener showing him inside the shed as if into a secret treasure trove. It was gloomy in there, musty and earthy, and there were cobwebs, and plant pots of all sizes, and an enormous watering can, and forks and hoes and rakes. He also remembered – of all things! – that there'd been complaints from the church warden that the shed looked ugly from the cemetery. Someone at the house must have eventually taken note of this and removed it. Planted the apple tree in its stead.

He bit into the apple. It was cold and crisp and not ready to be eaten, but the flavour brought back another apple, another day. One afternoon when he was nine or ten he and some pals had panicked some of the cattle on Cow Common, crushed a rabbit's head with a stone on the Coneygeare, and to finish a good day pushed through the gap in Mrs Kellaway's hedge, and torn apples off her trees. They'd taken a bite out of apple after apple, then chucked them, hoping she would see them from the house, which she did. And out she'd come, wielding a rolling pin and calling them all the names under the sun. They ran hell-for-leather, lobbing apples back at her, and as they ran Aldous bit into one, very deep, and thought it tasted wrong and paused to look at it. He'd bitten a maggot in half. The half that remained in the apple was still wriggling. He stood there spitting and spitting and spitting, and Mrs Kellaway caught up and set about him with the rolling pin. He kicked up his heels and got away with a few bruises, but he could taste that maggot for the rest of the day, and it was almost a year before he could bring himself to eat another apple.

Stepping back from the wall, Aldous's eyes fell on the one headstone he could never ignore. He knew the inscription and dates by heart, even though Alexandra Underwood had lived her entire life in his absence. But this time he found the epitaph changed. It was the other one. The unripe apple slipped from his hand as he read the familiar words and dates.

ALDOUS UNDERWOOD
BELOVED SON AND BROTHER
1934 — 45

It had happened again. When, he had no idea. Not that it mattered. Not really.

Friday: 4

Naia hoped she wouldn't meet anyone she would have to talk to. Morning breath, no mints in her pocket. But she seemed to be alone in the world: a blessing of the hour. Still no sign of the old man. Unsettling, given her plan to inspect his habitat. He might surprise her when she was poking about in there. In fact, though neither of them knew it, she had left Withern by the main gate just as Aldous passed it. They were unaware of one another because he had walked into a neighbouring reality half a dozen paces back, while thinking about last night's dream.

She waded along the bank, estimating that the water was a good ten centimetres lower than the last time she passed this way. Crossing the long bridge, Naia walked back along the opposite bank. She came to the first ragged trees, and hesitated, as at a door.

'Hello?'

No reply. Not that that signified much. He might have returned while she was on her way from the house to the gate. But she decided to chance it.

The thicket could only be entered by bending very low; passed through by strenuously avoiding the complex net of branches, twigs and barbs that tried to snag her or wound her every step of the way. It was flooded even here, an additional hazard she could have done without. As she stooped and dodged her way through, jabbed at from all sides, water slurping round her boots, she became aware of the birdsong. Glancing about from an ungainly crouch, she couldn't see a single bird, but it sounded as if there were dozens in there. Then she was through, and standing upright in the little clearing which Aldous had made his home.

The birds stopped singing.

Friday: 5

Aldous called them 'other lives'. There were three in all, besides his own. It was never his intention to enter them, it just happened, usually when he was distracted, or day-dreaming, or feeling a bit weary. One evening he returned to the thicket as usual and found all trace of himself gone, even the hammock. His first thought was that he'd had an unfriendly visitor who'd pitched his things out, but then he realised that at some point in the past few minutes he'd crossed into one of the other lives. There was no telling when it would happen. There was never any warning. Take the other day. First day after the rain stopped. Sunday? Monday? He wasn't sure. The days were all much the same to him. He'd been wading round the village, was passing the church when he felt the tiny jolt in the pit of his stomach that told him (when he was paying attention) that he'd crossed over. There was so little difference in his surroundings that he simply continued the way he'd been going. In minutes or an hour – there was no clearly defined duration – he would be back where he belonged, so he might as well go on.

He had entered the Coneygeare and was passing that ugly square building with the silly little balconies, the old folks' flats, when he saw some boys larking about near the bridge he planned to cross. As he started up the bridge he thought he recognised one of them, though he couldn't say where from. Seconds later it happened again. He lifted his foot, and when it came down he was on the same bridge in his own life, and the boys were gone.

There was never much chance of mixing the lives up, though sometimes he was fooled for a minute, like the day Mr Knight told him about Eric Hobb grown old. A red door on a house in one life might be blue in the others. Workmen might be fitting new windows in a bungalow in three lives but not the fourth. And people. Sometimes they knew him, sometimes not, because he'd met another version of them last time. He didn't like to speak to anyone unless spoken to. He wasn't that bold, that confident. It was such a strain talking to grown-ups. He hadn't the foggiest notion what they were talking about half the time. More than half.

The only people he really chatted to were the Mr Knights. In two of the lives there were no Mr Knights, unless he'd missed them, but that was fine. Easier to separate two than four. He'd talked at length to both of them. Sometimes he'd told them the same thing. Sometimes, for the fun of it, he'd given one of them a different story altogether. He had to be careful not to make a mistake later on when he did that. If occasionally muddled about who belonged to which life, he never had any doubt which was his. It was the only one without a gravestone with his name on it.

Friday: 6

It smelt awful in there. Like a public lav that hadn't been cleaned or disinfected for months. Litter floated on the water and an open tin box containing cheap personal possessions hung from a branch. She noticed a shaving mirror and a pair of scissors in the hammock. She hadn't thought of it before, but the old man was not clean-shaven. Not bearded exactly, but far from clean-shaven. By the look of it he didn't possess a razor, merely trimmed his beard hair as close to the bone as he could with scissors. She didn't feel right observing the relics and detritus of a man's life and was about to leave when she remembered the letters that he and his counterpart in her old reality had left in the message hole. They'd been written on a manual typewriter. So where was it? She poked about a bit, even felt under the water, but couldn't find it, and decided that he must keep it somewhere else.

Again about to depart, Naia remembered that this overgrown tract of boggy land had once belonged to Withern Rise. She stood at the heart of the two-hundred-yard stretch that Grandpa Rayner had leased way back to safeguard the view from the house. The Council had planned to clear the osier beds and develop the land for public use. If Rayner hadn't leased this wild stretch the view from the mid-sixties to the early nineties would have been right across Withy Meadows, with its benches and new trees and neat little bridges and picnickers and running dogs. Rayner leased his preferred view for thirty years – just long enough because, by the end of that time, the Meadows were obscured all along the river, the greenery having been allowed to grow back and flourish as it wished.

Naia stepped out of the thicket for a look at the house. She hadn't seen it for ages from this side. Years. It was almost a shock to see how dull it looked from here. Surely it used to look grander than that. It wasn't nearly as attractive as she'd always thought it, and it was smaller too. It was like looking at a different house. It was a different house to the one she'd grown up in, of course, but it should *look* the same, in all the essentials. Perhaps it was an age thing. Her age, not Withern's. Since leaving childhood behind she'd continued to think of the house, and see it, as it had seemed to her when she was younger, more impressionable, shorter. The view from here put a different perspective on the place. Not the best perspective, by any means. She might have a word with Kate about this. Kate had been at Withern Rise for just four months, but she loved it honestly and utterly. Naia knew she'd be open to suggestions for ways to improve it. In five minutes they would probably be talking about a complete makeover. Ivan would throw his hands in the air and go into one of his 'Have-you-any-idea-of-the-*cost*?' routines.

As Naia ducked out of the thicket she felt a small lurch inside, but, bent double, thought nothing of it. Straightening up on making her exit she heard a steady thrumming sound overhead. An enormous silver-white disc, slightly bulbous at the centre, with letters underneath which looked to her like Arabic, or Hebrew, was moving smoothly across the sky. Never having seen anything like it in real life, she might have stared until the disc met the horizon, but she'd continued walking while watching and suddenly her toe caught in a root, tipping her forward. Her arms plunged into water, followed by her knees.

'Damn and sod and *blast*!'

She got up, dripping. Returning her gaze to the sky she found that the peculiar craft had become a helicopter.

Friday: 7

Alaric needed information, and the only person likely to be able to supply it was Alex. 'You want to know about the Underwoods who lived here in the nineteen forties?' she repeated, with some surprise.

'Yes.'

'Why?'

'We had to do something at school about life just

after the war, and I've been wondering what it was like here then. For my grandparents.'

'Your grand*mother* didn't live here then. She was a child in Minnesota.'

'I mean Grandpa Rayner's side of the family. Didn't you look into them a while ago?'

'You know I did. For the family tree I can no longer lay my hands on, along with the album.'

'Album' was uttered with mild emphasis and a sharp look. He managed not to squirm, or give any sign of noticing the veiled accusation.

'So can you tell me anything?'

'I'm busy. Someone has to do this.'

She was cleaning the brass, of which there was an abundance, here in the River Room and throughout the house.

'No one would have to do it if you didn't buy so much of it.'

'I buy it because I like it.'

'So don't complain about cleaning it.'

'You sound like your father,' Alex said.

'No need to be insulting.' They had a small chuckle about this. Then Alaric said: 'Can't you tell me about them, even though you're so busy?'

'Not much to tell.' She continued polishing. 'I made some notes, linked some names, dug up a few dates, but I don't carry it all in my head. I kept most of the material, though. You could look through it yourself.'

'I'd rather you told me what you know, even if it isn't much.'

'Course you would. Because then you wouldn't have to do anything yourself. I've always loved research and reading, but to you and your dad such things are a chore. Must be a male thing. Or an Underwood.'

'Where did you put it?'

'Put what?'

'The stuff. Your notes and all.'

'The box room. In a suitcase.'

'There are a lot of suitcases in the box room. Which one?'

'It's an old brown job, near the front,' she said. 'I stuffed everything in an A4 envelope. Buff.'

'Buff?'

'The colour.'

He went up to the box room. The case was easy enough to find. He opened it. It smelt like a very small museum that only opens on Sundays, and contained plenty of things from the past that didn't interest him. One thing that did, marginally, was a newspaper clipping which seemed to have been simply dropped there, presumably by Alex.

Rail Victims to Wed

Two survivors of a railway disaster of February 2003 are to marry in Stamford today.

Ruby Patton, 27, and Bernard Walters, 32, were unknown to one another when their train came off the rails, claiming the lives of six.

They fell for one another in post-crash counselling. 'It was meant to be, I guess,' said Walters, an accountant.

The envelope he was looking for was attached by a thick elastic band to a slightly smaller cloth-bound book. He set the book aside and opened the envelope. There was a batch of papers inside, containing a quantity of notes and diagrams. Most of the notes were hand-written – in capitals, Alex's preferred way of writing. Easy as it was to read this, the information he sought was elusive. The names of known family members from the eighteen thirties to the present day had been listed and circled, with arrowed lines linking some of them. A few of the lines had been crossed out because the connections had subsequently proved false. There were also numerous memos on scraps of paper, envelopes and postcards, such as…

Gertrude Caldecott, origin unknown. Birth date 1867/8, music teacher. Nothing else found but married to Eldon. Check for date of marriage, Eldon's middle name.

Alaric's interest picked up when he came across the names Aldous, Ursula, Mimi and Rayner, along with their parents' names. But it was the date of death given for Aldous which shook him. 'Jesus Christ.' He sat back on his heels. He had no doubt that Aldous had died because of his own last visit, but Alex had done this research between the autumn of 2002 and Christmas 2004. The death was a recorded fact long before he'd caussed it. How did that work? How *could* it work?

He turned to the cloth-bound book that had been attached to the envelope. It was a diary, two-thirds full of small, precise handwriting. If the entries had been in English, he wouldn't have had the patience to read a page. As they were all in French –

L'eau est grise et bleue, large comme un bras de mer. — Un rayon blanc, tombant du haut ciel, anéantit cette comédie

– he didn't attempt a sentence. But inside the front cover he found several sheets of neatly word-processed text, in English. Even these didn't really interest him – much too much to wade through – and he was about to put them back when Alex said, over his shoulder: 'Translations of some of the entries by my friend Maureen.'

He jumped. 'How long have you been there?'

'Just came in. Thought you heard me.'

'Well, I didn't. Who's Maureen?'

'French tutor at the College. I have to assume her French is OK, seeing as she teaches it, but her English ain't so hot, know whadamean?'

'I thought you spoke French.'

'Enough to translate bits of a menu or a street sign, but that's about it. Maureen would have done more, found it fascinating she said, but she went off on maternity leave and thought she'd be rather occupied. This was written,' she added, dropping to her knees beside him and tapping the cover of the diary, 'by Marie Underwood, the French wife of your great-grandfather, who kindly lent *you* part of his name.'

'He needn't have bothered. Anything interesting in here?'

'Depends what you're looking for.'

'Anything about 1945. June, say.'

A quizzical glance. 'Suddenly specific, aren't we?'

He hedged. 'It just rings a bell. Something I heard. From you maybe.'

'I don't remember mentioning it,' Alex said, 'but in June 1945 there was a great tragedy in the family.'

'What tragedy?' he asked innocently.

She took the pages of translation from him and began riffling for a reference that had come to mind. Finding it, she read it out.

'"*Monday 18 June. Four days since it happened. The house is silent. The children keep to themselves. L says she will be leaving next week. Good riddance, I say. Alaric sits in the River Room hour after hour, or stands beneath the wretched tree, in the last of the water. How will he get over this? How will any of us?*"'

'Is that it?' Alaric asked when Alex paused.

'All that's relevant, yes.'

'Doesn't she say what happened?'

'No. Probably couldn't bring herself to describe it. Poor woman. My researches turned up the information that her eldest son died in an accident of some kind, but that's all that I have. His grave is in the cemetery over the back. Against the wall if you want to see it.'

Against the wall, he thought. Just like yours.

'Can I borrow these?'

'Course.'

He took the pages of translation and left her, still kneeling, picking at things in the suitcase. He went up to his room. Closing the door, he tossed the pages onto his bed and crossed to the side window overlooking the south garden. He couldn't see the Family Tree. His eyes were too full of tears.

Friday: 8

Naia had been too worn out last night to look at the retrieved album, and this morning her first idea on waking had been to visit Aldous's lair. She had time now, though. She slipped it from beneath her bed, turned to the back cover expecting to see the Underwood family tree, and found...nothing. It must have come unstuck, she thought, and turned back a few pages, hoping that someone had slipped it between them. Instead, she found blank page after blank page, preceded by picture after picture of Alaric instead of her. Disappointment that it wasn't her album battled with amazement as to why it had been where she found it. All she could think of was that Alaric had gone there sometime yesterday hoping she would also be there, so he could show it to her as a thing of interest. Finding that she wasn't there he had tucked the album into the branches and gone off exploring, but before he could return for it he'd been snatched back to the reality he'd set out from (which she refused to even *think* of as 'his').

She looked through the album from the beginning, fascinated to see all those photos that she'd only seen herself in till now. But how sad, coming to the end. No hint in the final pictures, as there couldn't be, that a world of smiling faces would end at the turn of a page, after which there would be nothing but blankness and emptiness. She thought of her own album. Mysteriously missing as it was, she still had the pages she'd removed from it; the pages that contained pictures of an Alex who, to everyone in this reality, had died before they were taken. Alaric might be glad of those pictures. If he had them, and added them to his album, he would no longer have to hide it away. Not that she would ever *dream* of parting with them.

She felt under her bed for the folder. Sitting on the floor, cross-legged, she went through the loose leaves to which, a few days before they parted forever, she'd seen her mother attach the most recent crop of prints. If she let Alaric have them she would never see them again. How fair would that be? He was better off than her now. Much better off. On the other hand…

On the other hand she could scan them. If she scanned them she would at least have a reasonable facsimile of them. She jumped up. She was alone in the house, so now was the perfect time. She went to the room Ivan called his office – in fact the smallest guest room – switched on his PC and scanner, and got to work.

In twenty minutes she'd scanned all the photos she needed to and transferred the images to DVD. As a backup, she created a password-protected file in her personal folder on the hard disk. Even then she was reluctant to part with the originals, but she bit the bullet and put the pages in Alaric's album. She then removed all the photos in which she figured, six in all. He'd have a problem explaining the gaps, but better that than trying to stump up a convincing reason why, in some pictures, he had such long hair, wore lipstick, a dress.

Even though she had copied them to hard disk and DVD, parting with the photographs was no easy matter. True, her mother, her dear, lost mother would get her pictures back, but there would be nothing of herself in them. Nothing to jog her mum's memory; make her think for a moment of the daughter she had born and been so close to for over sixteen years.

But then she had another idea. It wasn't much of one, but it went some way towards easing her sadness at giving up the pages. On half a dozen self-adhesive

Post-It notes she wrote a message to her mother, just three short lines, same message on each, which she stuck in the spaces where the photos of her had been. She knew that Alaric would see them first and remove them, but the act of writing the words and putting them in the book that was destined to rest in her mother's hands warmed her a little. Of course, there was a risk that Alaric would think the message was for him, but...well. She smiled at that.

All she had to do now was return the book to him. Which meant the 1945 reality, where she'd found it. Where he would inevitably look for it.

It started raining shortly before she was ready to leave: a soft, light drizzle of a kind she rather enjoyed as a rule; but she'd washed her hair earlier and rain would make it frizzy, so she put on her cagoule and tucked the album inside. Tugging the hood up she hoisted herself over the window ledge and stepped down into the water.

Friday: 9

He didn't read any more of the translations from Marie Underwood's diary that day. Alaric wasn't a great reader, even in a good cause. Besides, he couldn't sit still. The garden drew him. The Family Tree. He'd avoided going out all day, but by late afternoon he could resist no longer. Starting at some distance, he waded round and round the tree in slow decreasing circles. He had no intention of touching it today. Certainly not of climbing it. If he climbed the tree it might send him back to the day following Aldous's death. The body would have been found and cut down by then, but there would be things going on there that he wanted no part of.

A question came to him. If he'd visited a year that predated his birth, and that year was as current to its inhabitants as his was to him, what was the past if not another present? Did pieces of history break off and continue forever, unchanging, like closed bubbles of existence? Small eternities, you might say. There might be many of them, a great many, some linked to others by the equivalent of invisible strings, or timeholes, across decades, as this June seemed to be tied to June 1945. But wouldn't that make this month, or part of it, a small eternity too? If so, why? And why would it be linked to *that* year, *that* month? Because something similar had happened in each? What? Given that Withern Rise existed in both Junes, there was only one other major similarity that he could think of: the flooding. But there'd been floods in 1947 too, much worse floods, so why wasn't today linked to *that* year?

Perhaps the flooding alone was insufficient to bind two small eternities together. So what else was there that might do the trick? The only other notable event that took place at Withern Rise in June 1945, as far as he knew, was the death of young Aldous Underwood. But there'd been no similar death *this* June, at this Withern. He must be missing something.

Preoccupied, he barely noticed the tiny flash, like sunlight striking a window as you run past. He couldn't fail to notice, however, that he was no longer standing in water but sitting in the tree, in a profusion of leaves. Brighter leaves than the ones he'd been standing under seconds before.

Friday: 10

The transferral from Naia's tree to Aldous's had been just as quick and effortless as Alaric's, though unlike him she'd been ready for it. There, in the tree, she waited for the better part of twenty minutes with the photo album inside her cagoule. Twenty minutes which felt like forty. Here she was, at a Withern Rise of six decades ago, no idea how much longer she would have here, and she was just sitting there, doing absolutely nothing.

She eased herself into the water. It was a little lower

here too today. She ducked down to see as much as she could of the house. No movement in any window. No sign of activity at all. In fact, there was an unnaturally still and silent air about the whole property.

But then she heard a small sobbing sound. She tracked the source to the turf-covered hut near the kitchen, which she now knew to be an Anderson shelter. She crossed the space between the tree and the hut as rapidly as she could. As it wasn't raining here, she let her hood fall back. Reaching the shelter, she paused, listening. The leather sheet hung over the entrance, so she couldn't see who was crying inside. It was a young voice, slightly husky. She twitched a corner of the cover aside. There was no light in there, but the sobbing stopped at once. She pulled the leather further back. Light fell across the thin face of young Ray, sitting hunched up on a bench or table of some kind, barely clear of the water. He stared at her with big red eyes.

'Go away.'

'It's only me,' she said gently.

'Go 'way.'

'What's wrong? Why are you crying?'

He reached out and jerked the cover from her, returning himself to darkness, excluding her. She put her mouth close to the leather.

'My name's Naia,' she whispered, enunciating

carefully so that he would not mistake the name for any other.

'Don't care,' his muffled voice returned.

'You will one day,' she said.

'Leave me alone.' He began sobbing again.

She wished she could give him a hug, dry his eyes, find out what was upsetting him, soothe him better. But she had no right to do such things here. It was probably nothing anyway. He was very young. He'd probably been scolded by his mother for some mischief and was feeling sorry for himself. Still, she would have liked to comfort him. She recalled the times Grandpa Rayner had sat her on his knee when she was little. He used to hate to see her upset; went out of his way to make her feel better when she was feeling a bit down. He was a small man, asthmatic, with a wheezy chest that plagued him greatly during his final years, yet even then he was almost always cheerful, good-humoured, seeing the bright side. He liked to read to her at bedtime. Sometimes he would make up a story on the spot. Or sing some comic song. Grandpa Rayner, bless him. How he loved to sing.

With the photo album still inside her cagoule, she went on, past the hen house, feeling observed by a host of invisible eyes, to the partial cover of a fat hawthorn hedge whose white flowers seemed to be doing very nicely in spite of the flood conditions. There, feeling less exposed to the upper windows of the house, she gazed round the garden. There might never be another chance to see it like this and she wanted to take it in. There was a small wooden shed over by the cemetery wall, where she was used to seeing an apple tree, and parts of the garden seemed to be differently shaped going by the placement of the bushes and shrubs beginning to emerge from the water. The greenhouse in the middle of the kitchen garden struck a chord. They didn't have one themselves, but she was almost sure she remembered one from when she was small. What had happened to it? Could it possibly have been this very one, due to finally collapse half a century from now?

She continued surveying the garden from the hedge. Her eye was particularly taken, as it had been previously, by the many trees in the south garden, and the variety of them. The south garden of her experience contained just one tree, the rest being flat and empty, rather soulless. This one was full of them, and what a difference they made! She wasn't very knowledgeable about trees, but as well as the apple and the pear, with the rope hammock slung between them, she recognised an elm and three silver birches. Beyond these, right at the back, just within the boundary wall, a pair of evergreens, tall and dark and shapely, rose like enormous old-time Christmas trees. Many of these trees would have continued into her day if, a couple of years after the war, Withern hadn't been sold to barbarians who preferred a tennis court. Shame.

'Miss? Hello? Who are you? What's your business?'

She stepped out from the hedge, guiltily. A tall middle-aged man in waders much like her own leaned out of the open kitchen door. He was broad and rather gruff-looking.

'I was...looking for Aldous.'

An odd change came over the man. He gripped the doorjamb to steady himself, opened his mouth to respond in some way, but when nothing came out he stepped back and closed the door, sealing himself into the flooded kitchen. Staring at the blank door it came to Naia that there'd been something familiar about the man – the thick grey hair, the high-boned nose, broad jaw – and she remembered Mr Knight telling her that his father was gardener at Withern once upon a time. Well, she'd met him, and she hadn't been impressed.

She pulled her hood up, and immediately felt less vulnerable, less visible. She waded quickly across the garden, keen to put space between herself and the house.

•

Friday: 11

It was like sitting in a green cave. He could see nothing beyond it, but Alaric knew very well where he was; imagined he knew when. He'd been right here yesterday, just before he discovered the boy struggling for his life below. He was confused about other things, however. How had it happened? Why had he been conveyed or drawn here when he hadn't even been in his own tree?

He looked for the photo album he'd lodged in the branches yesterday. It wasn't there. Had someone climbed up and taken it? Had it dropped through the branches into the—

A movement below, beneath the mass of leaves that separated him from the water. He froze; listened intently. A blackbird peeked through the foliage, saw no threat in his immobility, and hopped onto the bough. He ignored the bird and the bird seemed willing to ignore him in return, as long as he did nothing hasty or untoward.

The blackbird even tolerated his cautious parting of the leaves to try and see who or what was down there, but when his knee slipped and his hands groped for something to hold onto, it leapt up and crashed away through the leaves. There was a reciprocal movement below, followed by a muffled cry. Alaric succeeded in creating a spyhole, and peered through. A boy swung by the neck from the lower bough. Aldous! So he wasn't dead! But again the polythene bag covered his head. Again he was suspended by the drawstring from that stump, flailing for his life. What the hell was he *playing* at?

Well, no time to go into that now. Holding onto the trunk with one hand, he pushed through the leaves legs first, feeling with his feet until they found adequate support. Then he lowered himself and moved along the bough until he was crouching above the frantic boy. Aldous looked up at him, eyes bulging with terror, the polythene stretched across his gasping mouth as one hand tried in vain to tug the cord from his neck. Undecided whether to tear the polythene and let some air in first, or pull him up by the collar to release him, Alaric, bent almost double, reached down. His fingers would decide at the instant of contact.

His hand was centimetres away when, with the slightest of lurches and a confusion of daylights, he was reaching for nothing, stooping in water beneath his own tree, and Aldous had been dead for sixty years.

Friday: 12

Water from the lane and the garden merged when Naia twisted the big iron ring and tugged the high green panelled gate back. She remembered a splintered, elderly version of this gate. It would remain in situ until the mid-nineties, when it would be scrapped in favour of a less substantial one which, three or four years on, would be vandalised and itself replaced – by a gate much more like this, but blue.

She pushed her way into the lane, pulled the gate to behind her, and stood, for the first time, beyond the rarefied precincts of the Withern Rise of 1945. As with the garden, differences were few but noticeable, the main one being the pair of seventeenth century cottages that had been demolished before she was born, to make way for the playground extension which she had skipped and played hopscotch in during her primary school years. They were unremarkable cottages, not particularly attractive, and there'd been few protests when they went. The tenants had been well-compensated and adequately rehoused. What Naia did not know was that the one on the left was the home of the Mr Knight she'd just met, his insecure wife Clarice, and their young son, who, many years from now, would present her with a white kitten she would name after her male double from another reality.

Still holding Alaric's photo album inside her cagoule, she headed up the lane towards the village, curious to see how it looked now. The war in Europe had just ended. The very war that she'd had to research and write about exhaustively in a recent school project.

Then, the period had been the dullest of the dull, but now that she was actually in it she wanted to see and experience every tiny detail. Mr Ackley, her excitable history teacher, would have given an arm to be here now.

From the outside, the main building of the red-brick, high-windowed mid-Victorian school was identical to the one Naia had attended until shortly before her twelfth birthday. It had to be different inside, though, all these years ago. She reached for the latch of the gate, intending to peer in a couple of the windows and see what a genuine nineteen-forties classroom looked like.

'Miss! This way!'

She glanced towards the voice. A man in a brown trilby was standing by the hedge at the end of the lane.

'Um…yes?'

'Don't move.'

'What?'

But by this time she hardly needed to ask. A wooden tripod stood in the water, an old-fashioned camera on top which was about to take a picture of the flooded lane, the school, her.

'Hold still, please.'

She stepped away from the gate, towards the man. It mustn't happen. She wasn't supposed to be here. She opened her mouth to tell him not to take the picture, raised her hand to cover her face.

The shutter clicked.

'Pictorial record of the floods!' the man explained. 'You might see it in the paper next week.' He lifted his tripod clear of the water and clamped the legs together. 'You're not from Withern Rise, by any chance?'

She couldn't speak. Couldn't think. The implications of that picture, so far out of time!

'Shocking business. Poor kid. Poor family.'

'Sorry, I don't...'

'Dreadful. Dreadful.'

The photographer waded off, dripping tripod against his shoulder like a rifle, along the road that within five years would be bordered by pebbledashed council houses. As she watched him go, Naia thought, *It's OK. No one will think twice about it. Just another photo. Forget it.*

Changing her mind about the school, she started along the village street. If it hadn't been filled with water she would have noted the absence of white lines along the middle of the road, single or double yellows below each kerb, but there would have been few other major differences. In the years between this day and her own, no building at this end of the street would be very greatly altered. It wasn't until she moved along a little way that small disparities became evident. The shop that in her Eynesford sold newspapers, magazines and confectionary bore the legend *Wm. Forrest, Grocer*, and opposite, on the other side of the street, a small blue door stood closed beside a modest window with a delicate little sign above it reading *J. Lee Fresh Bread & Cakes Daily*. Naia longed to go into the baker's and find out if fresh bread tasted different in the nineteen-forties, but she hadn't the right currency, or the ration book she might need to obtain the cheapest loaf or roll. Wading closer nevertheless, a small hand-written notice pinned to the door made it clear that she wouldn't have been able to buy much anyway.

> High waters has put out the ovens so no bread, sorry

She'd just finished reading this when a small jolt and a change of atmospheres compacted six decades into a couple of blinks. She was no longer looking at J. Lee the Baker's but at racks of bicycles behind a plate glass window in the Eynesford in which she had no choice but to reside these days. Just as suddenly, she was so weak, so incredibly weak, that she had no idea how she would ever make it back to the house.

Friday: 13

Alaric was so shattered this time that he thought he would die if he didn't lie down soon. He kicked his sandals off in the Long Room and left a trail of damp footprints all the way upstairs. In the bathroom, drying his legs with infinite weariness, he thought: *Houses half this size have two bathrooms. Not us. In a time-warp, us.*

He was on the way to his room, feeling his way like a shadow on the wall, when Alex saw him from below.

'Alaric, what on earth…?'

She rushed up, took his weight, helped him to his room, questioning all the way.

'Leave off,' he managed, 'I'm all right,' but she wasn't convinced.

'I'm calling the doctor.'

'Friday afternoon,' he said feebly. 'No surgery.'

'No. Damn.'

She stretched him out on his bed, leant anxiously over him.

'Is there anything you want to tell me?'

'It's nothing. Really.'

She felt his brow with the back of her hand. 'Can I get you anything?'

'Good dose of peace and quiet'd be nice.'

'I was thinking of a drink.'

'Go ahead. Just close the door behind you.'

She went downstairs, far more alarmed than she'd let on. She could think of no reason for him to be like that; felt useless, inadequate. A good mother would surely know what was wrong, and what to do about it, but she hadn't any idea at all. She couldn't push him, intrude too much, or she might alienate him completely. It had been touch and go anyway, until fairly recently. Of late he'd been a different boy: more light-hearted and affectionate than at any time since primary school. She'd put it down to maturity.

But now…if he'd been doing something to…

No. She didn't want to think about it. Didn't dare.

This time Alaric did not sleep, though sleep was all his body craved. Something had happened which needed to be thought through.

The only certainty was that he hadn't been transferred to the day after he found Aldous hanging from the tree, but to the same day, same time. This presented a conundrum. If it was the same day and time, why had he not met himself there? Come to that, why, yesterday, had he not found himself sharing a bough with the Alaric of today? Only one explanation seemed likely. Aldous should not have died and he'd been given a chance to put this right, *in another reality.* If he'd succeeded this time the boy would have lived on there, never to suspect that he had not done so elsewhere.

If he had succeeded.

Twice now he had failed to prevent the fatality that he himself had inadvertently caused. On both occasions he'd been withdrawn before he could manage it. Withdrawn? By what? *Sent* there by what? It was as if two incompatible forces were competing to stabilise, each in its own way, that point in 1945; that small eternity. One wanted him to stop Aldous dying before his due time; the other removed him as soon as it was able to because he didn't belong there.

He wondered. If he had twice entered the same point in time, and twice failed to save the boy, perhaps there'd be a third chance. And suddenly, he *wanted* another chance. These little jaunts did his health no good at all, but whatever the cost to himself he knew that he must, if the opportunity came, make a third stab at saving Aldous. He owed it to him. He *really* owed it to him. And next time he'd be ready. Next time he would not sit quietly among the leaves while the early stages of the death scene were played out below.

SATURDAY

Saturday: 1

Aldous's back hurt. Ruddy hammock. Feeble old carcass. And as if that wasn't enough, he'd woken with something nagging at his mind. Something about his gran. Whatever it was, it had not accompanied him into the waking world, but it disturbed him, this intangible truth. Truth? No. Couldn't be. He cast it aside. He would have none of it if it tarnished his few treasured memories of Gran. Her face came to him. Broad, fleshy, hair never quite tidy, dancing eyes, spectacles on her bobble of a nose when she was reading them stor...reading *him* stories. Him. Him. At bedtime.

He pulled his overcoat on, though it was already a warm day and looked like getting warmer. He turned the big collar up: a signal to himself, a command, not to entertain for a moment sly whispers of unthinkable things.

Saturday: 2

The water was so much lower today that Naia had been able, with some relief, to dispense with the unflattering waders. Green wellies instead. She slushed her way to the edge of the Coneygeare. It looked like a vast swamp now, with shoots of grass poking up here and there. She was wondering whether to cross it or turn around and go in another direction entirely when she saw Aldous, sitting on a bench in the middle. She dithered. They'd only spoken once, and she hadn't been that nice to him, but she did want to talk to him. Oh well, get it over with.

He was looking at a comic he'd found in the bin outside the chippie. A *Beano*. He liked comics. But hearing feet squelching closer, he thrust it out of sight. He was supposed to be an old man. Old men aren't expected to read comics. When he saw who it was he jumped up, intending to flee.

'No, wait!' Naia cried.

He sighed. Sat down again.

'Can I sit here a minute?'

'Free bench,' he said grudgingly.

She seated herself at the far end, two invisible people away.

'Do you remember me? We have met.'

'I remember.'

'I want to ask you something.'

'Oh yes.'

'Is your name really Underwood?'

'Did I say it was?'

'Yes.'

'Well there's your answer.'

'But it's my name too.'

'Well, well,' he said dismissively.

'Which suggests that we're related in some way.'

'Does it now.'

'But if we are…how?'

He looked at her for the first time since she sat down.

'You mean who am I? Where do I fit in?'

'Well. Yes.'

He turned away. 'Long story.'

'I'm in no hurry.'

'Why should I talk to you?' he said, still not looking.

'Because you've seen me before.'

'So you said.'

'I mean before that. A long time ago. When you were a boy.'

He glanced at her in surprise. 'When I was a *boy*?'

'Do you remember that far back?'

He laughed, without humour. 'Like it was yesterday.'

'And me?'

'You?'

'That's when you saw me, wasn't it? Me and someone else.'

'Don't know what you're talking about.'

'Oh, please,' she said, plaintively.

He hesitated, mulling, but then he looked her full in the face. There was something very childlike about him, she thought.

'What's this all about?'

'I want to know about you,' Naia said.

'Why? So you can have a laugh with your pals?'

She leant forward. 'I'd never do that. Believe me.'

And he did. It was impossible not to. He hesitated a little longer, but then gave in. Began to talk.

Saturday: 3

A bench on the Coneygeare. Alaric stabbed at the swampy ground with his heels, nervous about what he'd vowed to attempt if the chance came. The nervousness was partly of the deed itself, but also of the total loss of strength and energy afterwards. You'd think that it would reduce as the body got used to the process, but no, quite the reverse. Each homecoming was worse than the one before.

Having no explanation for this, he returned to his idea about the tightly-focussed periods of time he called small eternities. Being alone in that broad marshy space, just him on a bench, no distractions, his thoughts took off in a way they were not in the habit of doing. This was how Naia's mind worked sometimes, except that her imagination, less fettered by age and gender, did not need open spaces to fly.

Each small eternity, Alaric reasoned, might contain days or weeks of ordinary time but be complete in itself, like a knot in an endless length of string. Even though the boundaries of the small eternities were sealed, the inhabitants would not be stuck in them. Their lives would go on, day after day until their last, while the events of the significant period they'd left behind remained, self-contained and permanent – unreachable unless you were drawn there from another small eternity that shared a common factor. Common factor. Naia would be in her element with this. But what could the common factor *be* in their case? What event or characteristic could possibly bind this June to June nineteen forty-fi…

Oh. He had it. It was him. He had taken the polythene bag to the Withern Rise of 1945. That alone might not have been enough, but the bag had brought about a death that shouldn't have happened, so he'd been despatched to a duplicate reality, the same instant, to put things right. Only trouble was, he'd failed to save Aldous the second time too.

Wait a minute. If the focal point of the 1945 small eternity was Aldous's death and the events leading up to it, why had he been drawn there the first two times? He didn't take the bag until his third visit, and if he hadn't met Naia there he wouldn't have taken it at all. Come to that, if he had some part to play in the events of that June, why had Naia been there too? Did she also have a role in this, or was it merely because she just happened to be in her Family Tree when he was in his, so that they'd been drawn there more or less as—

Voices. Small, indistinct, but close. He looked about him. No one. The voices died, and at once it was as if they'd never existed. But he didn't simply shrug, and say, 'Oh, I'm hearing things now,' as most of us would. He knew very well that reality was not an impenetrable fortress. If, as Naia had once suggested, there was little or no space between the realities, it was a wonder more people didn't hear voices. To the ones he'd just heard he said, 'Hello?', feeling more than a bit foolish because he was completely alone. Expecting no reply, he was not disappointed.

•

Saturday: 4

'Did you hear something?' Naia said to Aldous on the bench in the Coneygeare.

'What sort of something?'

'I thought I heard a voice say "Hello".'

'You probably did.'

'Eh?'

'I hear them all the time. Visit them too.'

'Visit voices?'

'The speakers. Doing it a lot lately.' He tugged at his pocket. 'Aniseed ball?'

Naia declined. The tale he'd just told her was the saddest she'd ever heard, first-hand. What a tragic life. What a *short* life.

'You said there was someone else there. In the other bed.'

He crunched. 'There was more than one.'

'More than one bed?'

'More than one in the other bed. At different times. Over years, though it didn't seem like years to me.'

'But one in particular. You said there was one most of all. A boy. What was his name?'

'Um...not sure.'

She sensed that he knew the name well enough, and she was right. But it had only come to him while he was telling her about the particular occupant of the other bed.

'I think it was Tommy,' he said at last. There. It was out.

'How long was Tommy there?' Naia asked.

'Can't say. It's all mixed up.'

'Any idea how long ago? How recent?'

'No.'

'Did Tommy sleep a lot too?'

'Oh no, he was the opposite of me. Always awake. Tommy's problem was he couldn't sleep. That's why he was there, for them to find out why.'

'And did they?'

'If they did, they didn't wake me up to tell me.'

'Did you talk together, you and Tommy, when you were awake?'

'Well I couldn't have talked to him in my sleep, could I?' Naia smiled. 'If we talked I can't remember what ab...out...'

He'd trailed off. His eyes had become hooded.

'What is it? What's up?'

'I just remembered Tommy's visitor.'

'His visitor?'

He clenched his fists, withdrew into himself.

'What is it?' she asked again.

Instead of answering he stood up and stepped away.

'Going now.'

'Oh, don't.'

'Got to.'

With which he trudged away through the extended puddle that covered the Coneygeare.

Saturday: 5

It was a very ordinary rowing boat, but solid and heavy, far from easy to overturn on his own. When he managed to get it over, after much struggling, he fetched a bucket and began to scoop water out. He didn't get it all out, but having walked in water for days he could put up with a drop more sloshing round his ankles. He didn't care how uncomfortable it was; he needed to get his mind off the possibility of a further unscheduled trip to that fatal day.

He was about to lift a leg over the side when the light changed, and instead of climbing into the boat he was falling along the bough of a tree. His sudden appearance caused a blackbird, which had been thinking of stopping for a while, to change its mind. Alaric threw his arms round the bough to save himself, then lay still until he recovered his equilibrium and senses. Too slowly, in spite of his vow to be ready, he remembered how precious time was. Only then did he act. He tugged greenery apart. Aldous was there, hanging by the neck, feet kicking just above the water.

'Hold on!'

He jumped down, moved along the lower bough, reached.

Too late.

He was standing unsteadily in the water beside the rowing boat. He leant on the side trying to absorb what had happened. He hadn't even been *near* the tree this time; then, when he was there, it had all been over too soon. As he lamented his third failure to save the boy, every ounce of strength drained from him. In seconds, he was barely able to hold himself upright.

Saturday: 6

Naia was baffled. It had stopped her in her tracks when Aldous said it on the Coneygeare, but the conversation had moved on so quickly that she hadn't had time to digest it or ponder the implications. But it was evening now, and she was in her room, Alaric the cat on her lap, able to think.

She had wanted to know about the letters she'd found in two versions of the message hole, though she'd only asked him about one, believing that an alternative Aldous had placed the other. She'd had no doubt that this Aldous was the writer of the new one. Who else could it be? But he had frowned at the query.

'Message hole?'

'Yes, the…Oh.'

She realised that she hadn't seen a hole in the younger tree that he had known as a boy. It must have appeared some time later, when a bough broke off or was removed, leaving a cavity. But, as she soon learned, he wasn't merely ignorant of message holes. He claimed not to have left letters in any part of the tree in the present-day garden.

'Why would I do that?' he said.

'Well…to tell me things?'

'What things?'

'About…you know.' His expression told her that he did not. 'Are you saying that you haven't left typewritten letters for anyone, anywhere?'

'Typewritten letters?' Aldous said. 'I'd have to be able to type to do that. I've seen a typewriter, but I've never used one. Wouldn't know how.'

Saturday: 7

Alex and Ivan were at the shop, trying to repair the minor damage created by water that had seeped in the first night of the flooding. Ivan hoped to reopen for business on Monday. For Alaric, their absence was just as well, for the after-effects were the worst yet. It had been hard enough to find the energy to climb in through the window, but when he tried to get upstairs to his room the half-way platform was the furthest he could manage before his legs gave way. He lay curled on his side between the upper and lower floors for over an hour before his strength returned. When Alex and Ivan came home around seven, they found him brewing a mug of tea in the kitchen. 'Bit peaky again,' Alex observed. He told her not to fuss, and left them.

In his room he read some of the translation of Marie's diary. There wasn't much for some weeks after her son died. A pang of remorse shot through him. And shame. If he was right about a new reality being created each time he was offered the chance to save Aldous's life, it meant that there were now – or had been – two more grieving Marie Underwoods struggling to write diaries through tears. Two more small eternities in which a young boy had been found hanging from a tree with a mysterious bag over his head.

Saturday: 8

Aldous's denial of having written the letters left Naia with a new puzzle. If he wasn't responsible, who was? Already convinced that something dreadful had happened to the Aldous of 1945, she was now further convinced that at the point of death reality had bifurcated and another version of him had survived to become the old fellow she'd spoken to earlier. The remains in the grave and the old man belonged to different realities, but a letter that she had thought could only have come from him, or a version of him, had been left in the Family Tree of her old reality, where he died as a boy. If he was long dead there, how could he leave letters? The elderly Aldous of this reality had denied leaving a letter here, but someone had, just as someone who called himself Aldous U had left one in the other Family Tree.

Were there two more Aldous Underwoods? If so, why did they hide themselves? And what was their purpose in leaving the messages?

Saturday: 9

Later, while Alex and Ivan were watching a film, Alaric slipped out via a window in the River Room and waded round to the south garden. It was still light. At least three-quarters of an hour before it would start to get dark. He carried in his pocket the folding knife from the old boat-house. From now on, until he no longer needed it, he planned to have it with him at all times. The transition could happen wherever he was, and he wanted to be ready. Next time he would reach down at once and cut the cord round Aldous's neck. Then he would drop after him and rip the polythene from his face. He would be so quick, so efficient, that the power that seemed eager to withdraw him ever sooner would be outmanoeuvred. An Aldous Underwood would live on, and he himself would not be despatched to any version of that small eternity again. This, to him, seemed manageable and logical.

He went straight to the tree. He might not need to be near it for it to work, but he wanted to provoke the transfer so the deed could be done and he could put the whole thing behind him. He stood before the tree for some minutes until, fed up with waiting, he laid a palm on the trunk, inviting it to send him to that point in 1945.

Nothing.

So he began to climb.

He was half way to the bough upon which he planned to continue his vigil when he felt a surge of some kind beneath the bark, like blood pumping through a vein. Completing his climb at speed he threw his legs astride the bough. He put his hand on his pocket, felt the outline of the knife. He was ready. But there was no further movement, no change. He was not borne up within the branches. No carpet of leaves appeared below him.

He sat there for an age before impatience set in. Then, with the light fading, he clambered down; started back towards the house. He had gone less than a third of the way when it hit him that the water was higher than it had been forty-five minutes earlier. Surely it wasn't rising again. Seeking assurance that everything was as it should be, he glanced up at his bedroom window. To his surprise he saw someone there, a dark figure leaning against the glass. He paused, squinted, and…recognised himself.

Dumbfounded, he cast about for something that suggested a reality other than his own. Water level aside, it was all as it should be. Hang on. The water level. It was like this a few days ago. A few *days* ago? He jumped as though struck. There was movement about him, a very slight atmospheric change. Simultaneously, the water level dropped. He looked again at the window. No one there. But suddenly he was too tired to question, think or reason. He just wanted to get indoors. Get to bed.

Saturday: 10

It was pitch dark when it came to him. Lying in his hammock amid the trees, a bolt of lightning could not have shaken him more than the truth he'd been unwilling to allow. The cheery little woman who had sat him on the table to wash him when he was small, bathe him in the tin bath in front of the fire, brush his hair and read to him at bedtime: she was not his grandmother. Grandma Underwood died long before he was born, and he'd only met Grand-mère Montagnier a few times, when she'd visited from France, and the one time they went to her in Limoges just before the war. It was his mother who had washed him when he was little, probably brushed his hair too, though he couldn't remember her doing so, even now. Maman was affectionate but generally restrained, rarely jolly, and she'd read to him far less frequently than his father had.

No, the lovable woman he'd been thinking of so fondly these past months had been visiting Tommy, at the clinic. She was Tommy's gran, not his, and the visits might have taken place fifty or more years ago, while he himself was still physically a boy. Aldous remembered, now, finally, how each time he woke Tommy seemed a little older, and that his grandmother, who seemed not to age at all, was almost always sitting on a chair reading to him in that warm, melodic voice of hers, hoping to lull him to sleep. When she noticed that Aldous had stirred, Tommy's gran had always uttered his name, very tenderly, and moved her chair to include him in the reading. He had generally responded by promptly going back to sleep, with her face in his mind, her voice in his ears. At some point, one year, while Aldous was sleeping, Tommy was moved, and his gran had never been there again. Eventually, struggling to make sense of his life, mostly in his sleep, he had adopted her; fitted her into his brief, elusive past.

Somewhere nearby an owl taunted him. It was a long time before Aldous found sleep that night.

SUNDAY

Sunday: 1

The cat had gone walkabout again. Or swimabout. She'd looked everywhere for him, calling his name all round the garden. The last place she tried was the willow on the bank above the old boat-house.

Years ago, Grandpa Rayner had brought her here. She remembered him telling her that it was his secret place when he was a lad. Before his father died and his mother sold Withern to strangers, Rayner used to tuck himself away inside the willow, chuckling gleefully when they called from the house. He once hid there for an hour, he told her, and they were frantic by the time he emerged, big grin on his face. His mother had slapped his legs good and hard, but it had been worth it.

He told Naia something else about that bit of ground: that if you stood close to the trunk, and quite still, you could sometimes hear things. The one time he took her there in hope of demonstrating this, and the only other time she'd gone there, shortly after his death, she hadn't heard a thing. But today she was on a different mission. To find that wretched cat.

She was about to duck through the dense curtain of leaves when she remembered – as she often needed to remind herself – that she was not in the reality she'd grown up in. Some things were different here. Not many, but some. Perhaps the little Ray of this reality had not hidden under this tree, heard things here. The leaves brushed her softly as she entered, caught her hair, clung briefly to her cheek. A green veil fell about her. The light reduced, and the world, already quiet, fell utterly silent, as if a door had been covertly closed.

'Alaric? Alaric, where the hell are you?'

She couldn't see much. Certainly no cowering (or floating) bundle of white fur. She stepped closer to the willow's leaning trunk, still calling, into the circle of ground where nothing grew. She was standing there, calf-deep in water, when she heard a cat, mewing pitifully.

'Alaric, will you come *out*!'

The cat did not come out. But his cries ceased. Naia went cold. She left the willow in a hurry. The little devil could come back without her help. Or not. Up to him.

Sunday: 2

The barriers between the realities were breaking down. For him, at least. Alaric was sure of it. This morning, in the garden, he'd heard his name called, over and over again, and there'd been no one there. It was Naia's voice, small and distant but undoubtedly hers. He'd tried to track the source, but the voice kept moving, this way and that, until it faded to nothing. He could have done without that after lying awake half the night thinking about the two kinds of reality of which he had experience. He believed that to enter the parallel kind there had to be some level of emotional investment. Time-realities, small eternities, were something else again. Not surprising really because unlike parallel realities they weren't just next door, but fixed in past time – future time, too, for all he knew. If they summoned you, you had no choice but to go, and afterwards you were totally wiped out; more so each time.

And there was something else now. His impromptu trips were no longer confined to June 1945. Last night he had dropped, literally, from the Family Tree, into an earlier part of what he imagined to be his own small eternity. He remembered that evening well. Sunday. He'd been in his room, gazing out at the newly flooded south garden, when a figure had climbed down from the tree and started towards the house. But he hadn't seen an Alaric from another reality that night. He'd seen himself, six days on.

Sunday: 3

Four times in the past two days, Naia had climbed the Family Tree with Alaric's photo album in a carrier bag. The only way to get the album to him was to take it to 1945 and hope he'd be there too. She wasn't going to just leave it there for him to find at some point. It was far too precious to be dumped on the offchance. And, if she was honest, she wanted to see the expression on his face when he realised the extent of her sacrifice. She wanted his gratitude. Each time she climbed the tree, she sat on her usual bough waiting to be transferred to the younger version. Each time, she climbed down after half an hour with no such thing accomplished. At the third attempt she began to feel rather foolish, climbing trees at her age. So much so that she swore she would give it up if nothing happened at the fourth try. Come the fourth, nothing did. During the usual period of pointless waiting she became ill-tempered, then angry – at herself, the tree, the whole lousy business. She'd been so much better off before Alaric turned up the first time, back in

February. Until then she'd had no idea there was more than one reality; that the world was more complex than she'd ever dreamed. She'd been happier in her ignorance. And she'd still had her mother, her boyfriend, her *real* friends.

Vowing never to climb the tree again, and to settle for what little she had, she prepared to descend. She was surprised to feel a slight vibration under her hands, but the surprise was short-lived, for quite suddenly an excruciating pain leapt along her arms, exploded in her chest. A cry of agony was barely out of her mouth when the pain ceased. Unnerved, she lowered herself swiftly into the water, as if speed would ward off a reprise. In her haste, a pocket of her jeans caught. She looped the handles of the carrier bag over a branch and tugged herself free with both hands before completing her descent.

She was about to reclaim the bag when she saw something that took her breath away. The doors of the house and the garage should have been green, but they weren't. They'd been stripped back to the wood and stained. She was in her true reality, where her mother was alive. She didn't know whether to run to the house and claim it back, or...she had no idea what else.

Her response was decided for her when a man climbed out of a window of the Long Room. Her father.

Her real father. She wasn't ready for this. For him. She darted behind the tree. What would happen if she met her dad? Would there be a moment of limbo in which reality changed about them and she once again became part of his world, as if she'd never been away? If that happened, what of Alaric? Would he still have a place here? They couldn't *both* be here – could they? What if they suddenly became twins, sister and brother, recognised as such by just one mother, one father. Who would have the corner bedroom *then*?

Leaning against the tree, she felt a slight movement under her hands. Oh, no. No. She looked round the trunk, towards the house. The doors were green. She'd missed her chance. She could have howled. It wasn't *fair*. It wasn't bloody fair! But she held herself together, just about. She'd become quite adept at that. That and lying her arse off. She reached for the carrier she'd hooked over the branch. It wasn't there. It was still in the other reality, where Alaric the usurper couldn't fail to find it.

She moped for the rest of the morning, unable to shake her sense of failure and disappointment. She confined herself to her room for almost all of this time to avoid questions. Eventually, deciding that activity was the answer, she went outside, to the upended rowing boat by the River Room. She plunged her hands into the water, wormed her fingers under the rim, tried to lift it, not too successfully.

'Need assistance down there?'

Kate, leaning out of the window of the bedroom she shared with Ivan.

'Wouldn't say no.'

'Hang on then.'

Kate rarely wore anything on her feet inside the house now the weather was warmer, so she was already half prepared when she climbed out of the River Room window a minute later. Her faded blue chinos, cut off at the knee, completed the water-wading attire.

'Where are you thinking of going?' she asked as they hauled the boat up onto its side.

'Round the garden, while I can.'

Kate laughed. 'Nice idea.'

'Come with me,' Naia said. Company might be better than solitude.

'I would, but I've just been summoned to the shop.'

'What does he want?'

'Opinion on some Deco stuff he's just got in. He thinks he has a few Clarice Cliffs from the Griffin collection. If he has, they might end up in the house, but he doesn't know that yet.'

'I don't know how he ever managed without you,'

Naia said as they prepared to lower the boat gently into the water.

'Nor does he, but he'd never admit it.'

It proved too heavy to lower with ease, so by mutual agreement they stepped back to let it fall. The keel struck the water, which rose in a wave and drenched them both, to shrieks which quickly turned to riotous laughter. Then they stood looking at one another, hair in their eyes, pasted to their cheeks and necks, clothes clinging.

'That's obscene,' Naia said.

Kate looked down at the T-shirt which had just become a second skin. The picture on the front was of a computer. Underneath the computer were the words 'Byte Me!'

'What's obscene?'

'The decoration.'

Kate glanced from one nipple to the other. 'Oh, I don't know,' she said, 'I think they complete the motif rather well,' and thrust her chest out to emphasise this.

Again they shared hoots of laughter before going indoors to change. Twenty minutes later, Kate set off (in Wellingtons) for Ivan's shop in town. Naia, wearing her new bikini from Next for the first time, climbed into the boat. Nice day for a row round the garden half naked.

●

Sunday: 4

Alaric had planned to take the boat out before the end of the morning, but Alex had asked him to give her a hand moving furniture around: a favourite hobby of hers. The furniture-moving led to other tasks, the other tasks opened out into incidental supplementary chores, and the day loped by, so that it wasn't until late afternoon that he was able to get to the boat.

Parts of the garden north and north-east of the house were quite close to the surface now, so he could not row as freely as he would have liked but whenever he negotiated the great expanse of the south garden he kept well away from the Family Tree. Even though he knew it was no longer necessary to be near it, the tree made him uneasy. He felt the knife in his pocket.

Vigilant as he was for any eventuality, the rowing motion relaxed a part of his mind that did not need to be alert to sudden change. Thus he was able to return to his speculations about time-realities. So many momentous things had happened in the past two thousand-odd years, never mind the rest, that there might be as many small eternities as there were grains of sand in an egg-timer. He wondered if the only way into them was by 'invitation'. Also if you were always kicked out so soon after your arrival. And did you always have to go through that loss of strength afterwards?

Maybe you left your energy in the small eternity, like a fee for the privilege of being allowed in, or a toll.

Just a minute, though. Last night's visit to the previous Sunday hadn't drained him anything like as much as the other trips. He was very tired afterwards, but not so worn out that he could barely stand. Were the effects slighter because he'd only gone back a few days, to another part of his own small eternity instead of to a different one entirely? It couldn't be because he'd been there such a short time, because the last time he went to 1945 he was only there for a couple of minutes and he felt worse than ever on his return. He swore in frustration. How would he ever get the answers to such questions? There was no one to compare notes with, no reference book with an illuminating chapter that explained everything. There was just him, trying to work it out. Alone.

He had turned the boat towards the river and was crossing the still-submerged landing stage when, with no warning whatsoever beyond a shudder of light, he was in 1945 – and the tree. Shrugging off everything but the job in hand, he was instantly alert. It was going to happen again. But differently this time. This time he would *not* screw up.

•

Sunday: 5

Naia had spent the entire afternoon in the boat. At one point she moored outside the front door, climbed through the kitchen window, and after a quick dash upstairs for a pee, grabbed a bottle of Lucozade and put some cake in a sandwich bag. Then she was off again, rowing with languorous pleasure, pursuing a haphazard course, which amounted to no course at all, as happy as anyone can be in a world where they don't belong. She had a book with her, *The Autobiography of Alice B. Toklas*, and every now and then would stop rowing and sit reading in the quiet sunshine (wishing she'd brought *Cider With Rosie* instead).

Around four, she rowed along the drive, but got no further than the gate because the water barely covered the road now. She wasn't too disappointed about this. She'd been concerned about showing so much flesh in public. There might be boys about. She could have changed, of course, but it was a wonderful feeling, rowing around with the sun on her skin. She felt little need of company. There was only one person who would understand her preoccupations, and he wasn't here. Even with Alaric she might have felt self-conscious in her bikini. Not that he would look at her in *that* way. It was as unthinkable as her ogling his backside when he bent over. She grinned. She would never do that. Other bums maybe; not Alaric's. Wouldn't seem right.

Sunday: 6

A single glance told him that he was where he expected to be. Time being so much against him he squandered none of it, immediately easing himself, legs first, into the green expanse below. A blackbird looked in, saw activity, did not stop. Settling his feet on the lower bough, Alaric assessed the situation in a second. The boy had already fallen, startled not by an overhead flurry this time, but him, dropping out of the leaves. Again he wore the bag over his head. Again the drawstring had caught on the stump and tightened around his neck. His feet kicked just short of the water, and one arm flailed uselessly while the hand of the other tried to tug the cord from his throat.

Alaric took the knife from his pocket, inserted a thumbnail in the notch along the top of the blade, unfolded it. He reached for the length of cord between neck and tree, but the boy's frantic movements jerked it out of his hand.

'Hold on! Don't struggle!'

He snatched the cord, held it fast, began sawing with the knife. The blade was dull, so it was not as easy as he'd expected. Aldous's legs were kicking less wildly. His hands fluttered to his sides. Failure seemed likely yet again.

But then the cord snapped and Aldous dropped smoothly into the water. Yes! Alaric jumped after him. His feet hit the water, then the ground beneath. Steadying himself, he slipped one arm under the boy and raised him up, dipped the point of the knife into the heavy polythene, careful not to touch skin. The point was sharper than the blade, so a perforation was easily achieved, quickly converted into a gash. Without wasting time folding the knife and putting it away, he palmed the handle and tugged at the polythene with two fingers of that hand and the full frenzied complement of the other. The material tore easily now it was cut. Aldous's head was uncovered, but his face was lifeless, eyes closed. Alaric loosened the cord round his neck, yanked it away; threw it after the polythene remnants floating nearby.

'Come on,' he said, shaking the inert form. '*Come on!*'

Aldous's eyelids fluttered. As they did so, the light changed that merest fraction and Alaric was no longer holding him, keeping him afloat, but back on the river, in the boat, leaning dangerously. At once, as though a switch had been thrown, all the strength drained from him. All the energy. He toppled over the side, plunged down, the open knife still in his hand. Water filled his ears. He did not try to save himself. He couldn't. He was barely awake. The hand holding the knife struck bottom first; twisted at the wrist. The knife turned upward as his passive form reached it. The sharp point found a way between ribs, and, as the body slid slowly down the blade, met the heart and ran it through.

It was twenty past five in the afternoon when Alaric died.

Sunday: 7

At 5.19 Naia rowed across the landing stage. Another day, she thought, idling in the sunshine, and I'll be able to stand here again. She was happy enough about that. Might have sat there for some time, enjoying the light, the bobbing motion of the boat, if not for the spear of agony that pierced her heart without a whisper of warning. Her shoulders flew forward. She drew the oars sharply into her chest, sat as though frozen, enduring the pain for as long as it took, having no choice. It evaporated slowly, and when she sat upright again she did so cautiously, fearing its return if she moved too rapidly. Simultaneously raising her head she saw, less than a metre away, an empty rowing boat exactly like hers, rocking slightly, as if someone had just jumped from it, or fallen.

Then, like the agony, the boat was gone.

The same apparition was seen by an eleven-year-old boy at his bedroom window in a small eternity sixty years away. Surprised to see an empty boat on the water, he ran for his mother, brought her to see for herself. Too late.

In June 2005 Naia, not daring to speculate, even to wonder, rowed to the bank and the shallows. She climbed out. Her hands shook as she tethered the boat. Then she waded unsteadily round the side of the house, her fine, adventurous, solitary afternoon in ruins.

5.20pm. Birth and death. Snap. A pendulum stops in all small eternities of Withern Rise, where a Westminster clock stands on the mantelpiece. In more than one it is not restarted for two full years.

Sunday: 8

When the blade of Eldon Underwood's knife penetrated Alaric's heart, a new reality in which it was deflected by his falling body did not form. Realities are not always born of such moments. Duplication is not guaranteed. There are no absolutes, no fancy quantum principles. Chance rules. Aldous was luckier this time. Relatively. When Alaric was withdrawn from that small eternity, a vacuum briefly enclosed them both. But while Alaric was returned to his boat, Aldous passed through the three realities in which he had died this moment, returning in four heartbeats to the one in which he survived, where…

'Aldous! Aldous, what are you doing? What's happening there?'

Larissa did not waste time turning the boat around and rowing back. She stood up and jumped clumsily into the water. It was too shallow to swim properly now, so she waded to the tree as quickly as she could, with a great deal of splashing. She bent over him to make sure he was still breathing, and floated him to the house on his back. There she carried him into the kitchen and laid him on the table. For the first time since the flooding began, Marie came downstairs. She did not notice the discomfort. Ursula and Mimi were crying. Little Ray could only stare at his brother, so still, pale, deathlike.

Aldous could not be woken.

•

Sunday: 9

She'd been sleeping soundly, but suddenly she was wide awake, as if sensing someone in the room. She turned her bedside light on. She was alone, but then a heartfelt, sickening grief overtook her; a loss beyond her understanding that brought her into a sitting position on the side of the bed. There, a slow horror filled her. She jumped up, ran outside, started along the landing with dread. Mum! Something awful had happened to Mum! She reached the door of the master bedroom and was about to fling it open when she remembered everything, in a rush. The panic dissolved, like salt in warm water, but the grief remained. She retreated, shakily, intending to go back to her room, but passing the head of the stairs went down instead.

At the foot of the stairs she turned left, into the Long Room. It wasn't the room it had been when Alex was alive, but with Kate's flair and passion it was coming along. She drew the curtains back from the French windows. A high clear moon. Clouds like rags. She went to the couch, where she sat hugging a cushion, knees drawn up, gazing out at the gleaming south garden. Still something bothered her. Something she couldn't begin to identify. Perhaps it was the hour, the solitude, the insistent ticking of the clock, which had not stopped here.

She stayed there half the night, barely moving, thoughts drifting this way and that without focus or conclusion, fuelled by an overwhelming sorrow that made no sense at all. Drowsiness at last defeated her as the first birds stirred and light began to seep across the shallowing lake of the south garden. It was an effort, then, to leave the couch and walk the length of the room. From the lower hall, she climbed stairs which were suddenly very steep, to a room which, for once, did not feel quite her own. Yet she fell asleep immediately. Dreamt of a torrid affair with Orlando Bloom.

MONDAY

Monday: 1

Alex was in the kitchen, sitting at the table, staring at nothing. She vaguely heard the doorbell but did not stir. A pause, then Mr Knight appeared at the open window.

'Scuse, Alex, sorry to bother you, but I've just found this in the old oak, hanging from a branch.'

She got up. He handed the carrier bag through the window. Alex removed its contents; laid the photo album on the table. She sat down again, legs suddenly weak, fingertips tracing random patterns on the cover.

'You know, that tree's blighted,' Mr Knight said. 'Might not last much longer.' She wasn't listening. He felt for her. 'Like me to come in and make you a cuppa?'

She looked up. 'What?'

'Big mug of tea. Do you good.'

'No. Thanks.'

She wanted nothing. The light had gone out of her life. All she had left of her son was a photo album she couldn't bring herself to open.

Monday: 2

Ivan came home at lunch-time. He had something for Naia. Presenting it to her, he explained why he'd had to pretend he didn't know where it was. 'It was away being professionally bound. Cheap old cover before. I know how much it means to you, Nai. Wanted it to last. For you.'

She ran her palm over the expensive green calfskin. Tooled in gold near the top were the words: *Naia's Book*. It looked and felt superb, but it was all she could do not to shout at the man who thought he was her father. It wasn't the way Alex had left it. The way it ought to remain until it crumbled to dust. That was bad enough. But even worse, he'd done the unthinkable and had it covered with the skin of a young animal. He should have known that neither she nor her mother would have approved of that. Mistaking the tightening of her mouth and the brightness of her eyes for emotion and gratitude, Ivan did something that he rarely did. He put his arms round her and kissed her. While he was holding her, Naia glanced across at Kate. She knew at once that Kate understood how she felt, understood completely; that she too was saddened by what Ivan had done, but didn't want to let on.

Kate. Dear Kate. These past few months they'd become close without even trying. Kate had told her a great deal about her life, her interests, her past loves, and in return Naia had told her as much as she felt able to about herself. She said nothing about other realities and not belonging to this one; nothing about a boy who shared a name with her cat. Just told her enough to seem normal.

After lunch, when Ivan had gone back to the shop, she told Kate about Aldous; his tragic life; that she believed him to be her great-uncle; that he was homeless, living out of doors. Kate asked to meet him.

'Oh, he could be anywhere,' Naia said.

'He might be just around the corner,' said Kate.

They set off to look for him.

In the drive, rounding the curve to the main gate, they saw a man looking through the bushes at the house. Not just looking. He was taking photographs. As the water muffled their footsteps he hadn't heard them coming. They stopped to watch him.

'What's he up to?' Kate whispered.

'I don't know, but I think I saw him the other day. I'm sure it was him. He was just standing there, looking at the house. Through binoculars.'

'Binoculars?'

'Yes. Meant to tell you.'

'I wish you had.'

Kate started forward, simultaneously raising her voice. 'Hello there! What's this?'

The man jumped at the sound of her voice; immediately flummoxed, embarrassed.

'S-s-s-sorry,' he stammered. 'J-j-just taking p-p-pict...'

He turned away rather than attempt a conclusion; fled up the drive.

'Dodgy,' Kate said.

'Think we should tell the police, just in case?'

They decided to do so, but a few minutes later bumped into Aldous by chance, and forgot. After talking to him, Kate observed that he was an 'odd one'.

'I'd be pretty odd myself if I'd had a life like his,' Naia said.

'Yes. Nai?'

'What?'

'We have quite a big house. Two spare rooms...'

'You mean...?'

'Just a thought.'

It was precisely the thought Naia had hoped she would have. But she needed clarification.

'You mean bring him to Withern? To live?'

'If he wants to,' Kate said.

'He might not.'

'No, but he might be glad of the choice. I mean it seems only right. Him being a relative and all. Of yours. Your dad's.'

'Dad would never agree.'

'Oh, I'm sure we could wear him down between us. He's only a man, after all.'

Later they put it to Ivan. He resisted, fiercely, but Kate carried on as if he hadn't spoken. Just like Mum, Naia thought. And gradually, reluctantly, for the sake of a quiet life, he came round – to an extent.

'I'm not having him upstairs. You think I want to go to the bathroom in the middle of the night and meet some cracked old geezer on the landing?'

'He might not be too keen on meeting you in your boxers in the middle of the night,' Kate said.

'He won't have to, 'cos it's not gonna happen.'

'Well what do you suggest?'

'I'm not suggesting anything. I don't want him in the house, dammit.'

'We could convert the dining room into a bedsit,' Naia said.

'Oh yes? And where would we eat?'

'The River Room, like we do now.'

'We only eat in the River Room in summer.'

'We can eat there all year round just as easily.'

'The River Room's a long way from the kitchen,' he pointed out.

'So we buy roller skates.'

'He'll still want to use the bathroom. Which means he'll be going upstairs.'

'I have an idea about that,' Kate said.

He frowned. She told him her idea. He wasn't impressed. 'Oh yeah, sure, like I'm made of money.'

'Business is picking up,' she reminded him.

'Thanks to Kate,' said Naia brightly.

His frown became a scowl. He had no intention of giving in gracefully.

'I can't believe I'm going along with this,' he said. 'You two are asking me to disrupt my life for an old codger I've never met. Never even heard of till now.'

'Yes, odd that,' Kate said. 'You'd think someone in your family would have mentioned his *existence*, if nothing else.'

'Exactly. How do we know he's who he claims to be?'

'I know,' Naia said quietly.

'How do you know?'

'I know.'

And that was that.

ANOTHER DAY

Naia wasn't entirely surprised when Aldous said that
he didn't want to live in the house. He was tempted
by the garden, though.

'We could get you a tent, if you like,' she said.

'A tent?' He wasn't sure. Might still feel hemmed in
by a tent. He said as much.

'Well there's always the Family Tree,' she suggested.

He looked puzzled. They were in the garden at the
time, so she was able to point it out to him.

'Is that what you call it? The Family Tree?'

'Yes. You could camp under it. Or in it. Get you a
ladder.'

'No,' he said. 'Not there. But that's a nice big willow
down by the bank there. Wouldn't mind that.'

'It's possible,' Naia said. 'And perhaps we could rig up
some sort of waterproof covering to keep the rain out.'

'That'd be nice.'

'Pretty cold in winter, though.'

'I'll survive. Only thing is...'

'What?'

'If I get caught short.'

She told him about Kate's plan to convert the utility room next to the kitchen into a bathroom. 'There's a side door from the garden,' she added. 'You'll have your own key, and if you get hungry or thirsty the kitchen's just another door away.'

She saw his eyes light up in that boyish way they did sometimes, then narrow as he struggled to give the impression of pondering the proposition, in an elderly sort of way. Then he nodded slowly, as if to say that after due consideration he'd come to the conclusion that he might, perhaps, be able to stand being indoors for a few minutes at a time, in his own bathroom, and that he might even manage, at a push, to pop into the kitchen for the odd bite or sip or something. So long as he didn't have to *stay* there.

And so it was settled. Aldous Underwood was coming home.

ANOTHER NIGHT

Alex sat on the bed in the room that had been Alaric's, looking, for the first time, through the photo album he'd denied knowledge of for months. The family tree she'd spent so much time compiling wasn't inside the back cover, or anywhere else, but this was a small thing. What mattered – and even this didn't matter very much – was that he'd kept the book from her all this time. Why? And why had he left it at the Family Tree? She sighed heavily. He must have had his reasons.

She turned another page. It broke her heart to look through the album, his life, but it was all there was now. Ivan sat elsewhere in the house, nursing the grief in his own way. They could no longer look one another in the eye. Things would never be the same between them after this. How could they be? Their only child was gone. Their boy. His life cut short before he'd had a chance to do anything with it. Before he'd lived at all, really.

The thick pages turned automatically in her hands. She saw the pictures, yet saw none of them – until she came to the last few pages. There she found that every photo that had featured Alaric since the middle of 2003 had been replaced by a little yellow note, with writing on it. His writing. Same ten words on every one.

> I love you.
> I miss you.
> Think of me sometimes.

She didn't understand. Why had he removed the pictures of himself and stuck these notes in? Written these words? He couldn't have known it was going to happen, couldn't have *intended* it…could he? She read the three short sentences over and over, until, finally, the breath rushed out of her, her head fell forward, and she was sobbing into her hands.

'Alaric. Oh, Alaric. My love.'

So immeasurable was her grief that it could not be contained within a single reality, or even the bounds of time. Her misery was of such intensity that it was instantly complete and indestructible, another small eternity which would always exist, and occasionally, on certain nights at this hour, be witnessed by those of her blood who shared a particular disposition and sensibility.

In one reality a teenage boy who'd gone to bed early because he could find no reason to stay up, was woken by the infinite sorrow. Opening his eyes, he half expected to find someone crying on his bed. There was no one, so he imagined that he'd had an especially vivid dream, but all next day he carried within him a very deep sorrow, which returned him all over again to his great loss. That was the day he resolved to try and find a way to reach, once more, the reality in which his mother lived on.

But not yet. He wasn't ready yet. Soon perhaps.

Soon.

You have just read

SMALL ETERNITIES

— some additional background
material follows.

THE YEARS BETWEEN

ALDOUS UNDERWOOD:
A Life

The normal human brain contains thousands of cells that manufacture the chemical Arexin, which wakes us and keeps us awake for hours each day by periodically stimulating the brain. Without Arexin we might sleep our lives away. Aldous's near-death ordeal at the age of eleven, followed by the unconscious scramble through three conjoined realities in which he actually did die, nullified all but five percent of the Arexin cells in his brain. Arexin-deficient to an unnatural degree, he was unable to stay awake. In the decades following the accident that almost killed him, the sleeping Aldous dreamt a great deal. Often, the dreams concerned Withern Rise, family, friends, and two strangers in a tree; but on waking he always remembered as little of his dreams as of his life.

He was nearly seventy by the time medical science had advanced sufficiently for his disorder to be identified and drugs be developed to simulate the waking action of the dead brain cells. Before long he was able to remain conscious for hours each day, falling gently asleep around dusk and waking with the light.

As a regular sleep-wake pattern established itself, a programme of exercise and physiotherapy was introduced to restore his body's flexibility and strength. He was required to sit up in order to regain his sense of balance, stand in a support frame, walk in splints between parallel bars to fortify his lower limbs and spine. Muscle-building hydrotherapy was an unexpected pleasure, though he hated the neck support he was forced to wear until his neck strengthened.

After almost six decades in bed he was surprisingly fit after just eighteen months' treatment – a recovery undoubtedly aided by a mind that had not aged with his body. An educationalist who specialised in helping slow and reluctant learners was brought in to help him 'grow up' and learn something of society and the world that had developed while he slept. He was a willing student, if a naïve and frequently confused one, frustrated by his memory's reluctance to return other than in bits and pieces. One very powerful image did come back, however. The house he knew as a boy. But he had no knowledge of its whereabouts, and contact with surviving relatives had been lost since Marie died. The name and location of his childhood home were discovered by Lucy Fry, his amiable tutor. The information thrilled him. The only life of which he had any memory, slight as it was, had occurred there, and he was eager to see it again. There, he was sure, the rest of his memories would reveal themselves to him.

Aldous returned to Eynesford in February 2005. There, as his memories grudgingly came back, he discovered an ability to enter (whether he wanted to or not) realities other than his own, his 'other lives'. There were three in all. Three in which, in each cemetery behind the house, there was a headstone bearing the name that he'd learnt was his. There were other small differences in the four realities, but there was one thing that did not change: there was no place for him at his childhood home. The best he could do was live nearby.

He didn't mind not living at the house. In any house. On leaving the clinic a complex new world had opened out before him; four versions of it as it turned out. Free of his narrow, iron-framed bed, of medical staff and exercise regimes, the thought of being cooped up again made him nervous. After all those years of waking to the same walls, an unchanging ceiling, living indoors would be like having his head shoved into a bag of some sort, gasping for breath.

THE RECOVERY OF WITHERN RISE

When Rayner Underwood was a young boy he could stand on Withern's landing stage and look to left and right and see nothing but an impenetrable mass of foliage and leaning trunks. The river was decked with water lilies then, crowned with yellow and white flowers, through which small boats had a hard time progressing. Rayner was seven at the time of the tragedy, nine when they moved away. He hated the place they moved to, the ugly little prefab with its tiny treeless yard, no river within an hour's walk. He missed Withern Rise terribly. He'd been born there. He'd taken his first steps there, had his first falls and upsets there, first Christmases, Easters, birthdays. He'd heard his first songs there, from his father's lips. Until he started school Withern was his whole world. At the age of fourteen, he vowed to bring that world back into Underwood hands as soon as could be managed.

Shortly after his sixteenth birthday he left home to become assistant to an antiquarian bookseller in Trinity Street, Cambridge. His employer Garrod Nesbit, who had no children, died in 1959, leaving Rayner the gloomy little premises he liked to call his shop. *Garrod's Antiquariana (Books)* was not a very profitable concern, and Rayner would never have made his fortune there in the normal course of business; but in 1961 he made the acquaintance of two ladies seeking a purchaser for a centuries'-old volume that had recently come into their hands. This little book, hand-written in an unfamiliar language, copiously illustrated, was known by the name of the dealer who had owned it since 1912. Rayner immediately saw the potential of the Voynich Manuscript and sold it, through contacts, to rare book dealer Hans P. Kraus of New York for $24,500. The deal not only brought him a useful handling fee but a paragraph or two of minor fame, which he turned to his advantage when seeking finance for the purchase of Withern Rise. These paragraphs also brought him raven-haired twenty-one-year-old Betty Joyce Arnott of St. Paul, Minnesota, who had recently discovered the poetry of his grandfather, E.C. Underwood. The couple moved into Withern Rise in September 1963 and married the following spring.

The only blight on this new phase of Rayner's life was threatened in 1964 when Stone Parish Council announced that the osier beds were to be drained, cleared and landscaped for public use and recreation. Horrified by the prospect of losing his gloriously unruly view, Rayner managed to acquire sufficient additional funds to lease, for a period of thirty years, the two-hundred-yard stretch of marshy bank directly across from the house.

The view secured, the next item on his agenda was the oak tree in the south garden. He remembered all too well the dreadful day twenty years earlier when his big brother had come to such grief beneath it. It still made him shudder to think of it. Rayner contemplated his choices. Should he cut the tree down? Would its removal dilute the memory of that appalling episode? Eventually deciding that the tree should go, he made the arrangements, but the morning the work was to have begun he had second thoughts. The tree had been there for six full decades, growing tall, filling out, reaching maturity. It was part of Withern Rise. Besides, it was all that was left of the trees of the south garden, cleared away by the family that had owned it since the forties. No, it must stay. But there was something he could do. One little thing that might ease the pain when people commented on its grandeur, its majesty. He could rename it. And so he did. From that day forth it was no longer referred to as Aldous's Oak, but as the Family Tree.

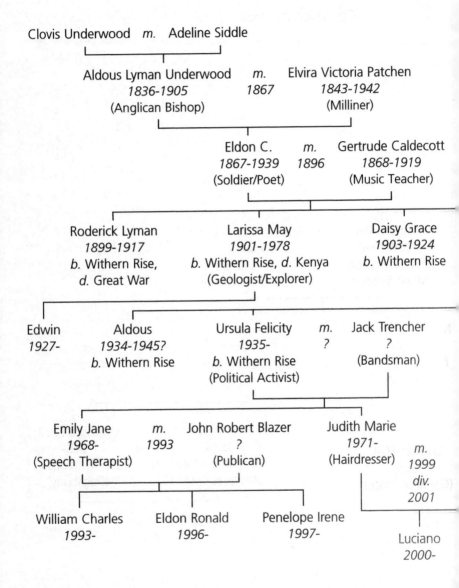

Clovis Underwood *m.* Adeline Siddle

Aldous Lyman Underwood *m.* Elvira Victoria Patchen
1836-1905 *1867* *1843-1942*
(Anglican Bishop) (Milliner)

Eldon C. *m.* Gertrude Caldecott
1867-1939 *1896* *1868-1919*
(Soldier/Poet) (Music Teacher)

Roderick Lyman Larissa May Daisy Grace
1899-1917 *1901-1978* *1903-1924*
b. Withern Rise, *b.* Withern Rise, *d.* Kenya *b.* Withern Rise
d. Great War (Geologist/Explorer)

Edwin Aldous Ursula Felicity *m.* Jack Trencher
1927- *1934-1945?* *1935-* *?* *?*
b. Withern Rise *b.* Withern Rise (Bandsman)
(Political Activist)

Emily Jane *m.* John Robert Blazer Judith Marie
1968- *1993* *?* *1971-*
(Speech Therapist) (Publican) (Hairdresser) *m.*
1999
div.
2001

William Charles Eldon Ronald Penelope Irene
1993- *1996-* *1997-*
Luciano
2000-

The Underwood Family Tree

Compiled by Alex Underwood, 2004

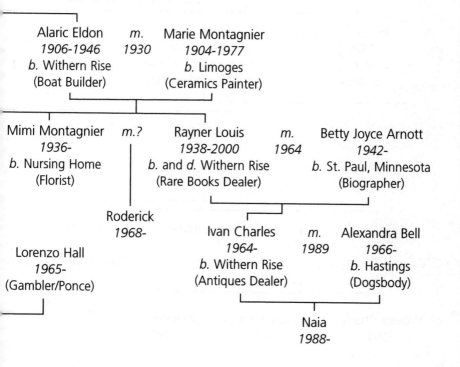

Alaric Eldon   *m.*   Marie Montagnier
1906-1946   *1930*   *1904-1977*
b. Withern Rise   *b.* Limoges
(Boat Builder)   (Ceramics Painter)

Mimi Montagnier   *m.?*   Rayner Louis   *m.*   Betty Joyce Arnott
1936-   *1938-2000*   *1964*   *1942-*
b. Nursing Home   *b.* and *d.* Withern Rise   *b.* St. Paul, Minnesota
(Florist)   (Rare Books Dealer)   (Biographer)

Roderick
1968-

Ivan Charles   *m.*   Alexandra Bell
Lorenzo Hall   *1964-*   *1989*   *1966-*
1965-   *b.* Withern Rise   *b.* Hastings
(Gambler/Ponce)   (Antiques Dealer)   (Dogsbody)

Naia
1988-

In THE UNDERWOOD SEE, the final part of The Aldous Lexicon, four more months have passed. It is October. The Family Tree is dying. In one reality Withern Rise is up for sale. In another, a seventeen-year-old savage who refuses to answer to the name of Alaric Underwood plans wholesale destruction — and the death of a man who calls himself Aldous U.